Beloved Monsters

Story of Perilous Crossings

Kamran Nomani

ISBN-13: 9781980422426

DEDICATION

For my love and my best friend

My wife

Farzaneh

DEDICATION

For my Daughter

Leila

"My love for you shall live forever"

Chapter 1

The Plan

When I look back at the tumultuous early part of my life, I can clearly see I am here today because of what happened to me and my family that dark summer night of 1981 in Tehran.

It started like any other night. The somber, faded voice of a muezzin at the mosque drifted over the rooftops, inviting the faithful to prayers as the sun settled into a smog-laden horizon. The hazy air was warm and dirty in the busy district of western Tehran where we lived. The entire country was aware we were at war with Iraq, but we all thought that were far enough away from the front lines and safe. Only the economic effects of the war were expected to touch us directly here in the capital. Although we practiced often for a possible air raid, no one imagined Iraqi planes would dare fly this far inland to bomb our city

My dad had just finished preparing dinner and the aroma of his latest combination made our mouths water.

"Time for dinner, everyone," he called through the house.

Walking into the dining room, we were greeted by his gentle smile. I always thought that dinner table was his one peaceful domain after all the humiliation, violence, and devastation he'd experienced in life. It was a place where he could count his blessings and be proud of the fact that he had his family around the table. I could see in his kind face that he was content with his life as a loving husband and a caring, attentive father.

That fateful night was anything but a peaceful family evening for us, or anybody else in the capital. Everyone had a chance to take their places around the table and begin taking our first bites when the lights suddenly snapped off. The chilling sound of the sirens sent tremors through our bodies and froze us into place. This was nothing like any of the drills we'd had before. None of us felt prepared or seemed to know what to do. We had no idea what was really going on. Were we actually under air raid or was this just an unusual test? Could this be true? Had war finally managed to come to our homes?

We could hear the scrape of his chair as my father jumped out of his seat.

"I'd like you all to follow me to the basement now," he calmly asked us. "Follow me."

However, we stayed frozen in place. None of us could think straight as we heard the real sounds of explosions taking place in the background all around us. It was absolutely dark in the house and we worried about making noise, thinking, irrationally, it would attract the bombs to our home.

A lighter lit up the air at the head of the table, illuminating my father's face.

"I need you to move, now. Come with me to the basement."

His spark of light and calm but firm voice finally got us moving. We all went down the stairs to the basement and out to the backyard through a little door created just for this purpose. I vividly remember the sight of flying bullets brightening the night sky from all angles as we made our way to the basement. I knew they were anti-aircraft guns, but they seemed to be shooting aimlessly all over the dark sky without making any contact with our attackers. They made a loud bang each time they were fired, filling the night with terrifying sounds.

I could also hear people yelling at the cars on the streets nearby.

"Turn off the lights, turn off your damn lights!"

The bullets were still flying, and the noise was deafening as targets on both sides were hit. The rumbling and crashing of war went on for 30 minutes all around us before the sound of the sirens suddenly stopped. A deafening silence filled up the space. We all held our breaths. I could hear my heart pounding and saw my dad looking at me with reassurance, but I could also see the helplessness in his otherwise calm eyes. He looked up at the sky and covered my sister's head with his one hand, cradling her to his chest. My mom was quietly crying, and my little brother was latched on to her legs.

With the suddenness of a lightning flash, the sky brightened up again in rows of bullets. Within seconds, the deafening sound of explosions again came from every direction. It seemed it had somehow become easier to zero in on specific targets. I closed my eyes, realizing our house was possibly even more vulnerable this time. I took a big breath and grabbed my father's other hand. I could smell sulfur in the air and had the bitter taste of fear in my mouth, but I didn't care. I was holding my father's hand and we were all together.

That hot summer night of 1981 in the northwest district of Tehran was no longer dark, for it was illuminated by the flashes of explosions, the fires raging in targets struck, and anti-aircraft flares flying in blind directions trying vainly to shoot down the invisible planes that were attacking us. That night was the beginning of my life's real journey. The war between Iran and Iraq broke out two years prior, but this was the first time the capital was getting a taste of real war. I was only 19, but I'd already had a share of it myself.

I was born as an army brat, so most of my life was summarized in episodes of moving from one army camp to another with my family. My father's job in the army and his continued rise through the ranks of the military kept us on the move every two years or so. I could never count on a long-term friendship since we knew we would never be in any of those places for more than a few short years. As a result, I never developed a sense of belonging to any particular place. There was nowhere I could really call home, nothing but my family to protect. Protecting my family was something I'd learned to do the gloomy, cold winter of 1978, during the beginning of Iran's Islamic revolution.

In that year, we were attacked by Kurdish militia and disgruntled solders at the army base we lived in located in the northwest corner of Iran. Our house, amongst many others on the base, was set on fire. I was only sixteen when I learned to use a Kalashnikov rifle and helped guard our family and community next to my dad, other army personnel, and members of their families. Our lives were transformed from an easy-going Western style of living on the army base into a horrible nightmare in a matter of weeks. Within a month, we found ourselves in an all-out warzone where everyone wanted to kill us and burn our belongings. Our entire community was devastated, however, the sheer survival instinct and strength demonstrated as we all learned how to quickly adapt to the new situation still amazes me when I think back on it.

My family moved into the capital soon after those dramatic events and, thanks to my mother's financial skills, we purchased a house in a decent part of town. She had every reason to be proud of her contributions. She was only 16 when she married my dad. He was 13 years older than her, but that didn't stop them from loving each other unconditionally and forever. Almost immediately after the wedding, my mother got pregnant with my sister and couldn't finish high school. I was born soon after that and it looked like her dreams of a career for herself were over. As soon as my sister and I were a little older, though, she went back to school. I can't comprehend the determination it would take for her to finish high school and then college having two little kids and being a fulltime homemaker. It took her many years, but by the time my sister and I were in middle school, she'd graduated from college and became a schoolteacher. Soon after, my youngest brother was born, but that didn't stop her from going to work every day.

The day we moved to the capital, we all benefitted from her tireless studies and hard work. We could never afford such a nice house with only my dad's salary. We were happy again. Our first big house and we were here to stay, far away from the direct effects we might expect from the war.

By the time we settled in the capital city, the revolutionary government was in full force and was installing all new Islamic laws throughout the land. We, like every other family that wanted to survive, conformed to the new strict rules and regulations of the regime. Dad had worked his way to the rank of an army colonel in the previous regime after more than thirty years of dedicated service, but he was dismissed from the army just a few months after we arrived in Tehran. He was later arrested, prosecuted, and even put in prison for a short period of time. His passport was taken away from him and he was also under house arrest for a while. These events left him broken and humiliated. He never emotionally recovered and fell into a long depression. Our short-lived happy days were over.

During those dark days, my mother worked as a teacher and supported the family. My siblings and I went to school in a robot-like haze every day and witnessed a variety of government-led atrocities and unbelievable scenes. We saw regular people being chased, arrested, and shot by the revolutionary guards on the streets for no apparent reason or, when reasons were given, they seemed illogical or out of character. One rainy, cold, winter day, as my sister, brother, and I were heading off to school, we witnessed in shock the hanging of the 16-year-old next door neighbor. My sister covered my little brother's eyes and started crying. I wanted to drag both of them out of the crowds and away from that disturbing scene, but I could not move a muscle.

"He was obviously a communist," I heard one of the other witnesses in the street say, but he didn't sound terribly convinced.

Days like that shaped the deep hatred I still have for that government and its agents. I believe I will carry that hatred in my mind and soul for the rest of my life.

In those years, we learned how to stay quiet. We learned how to see unfairness, cruelty, and oppression and say or do nothing. We all learned how to get in long lines to get our daily needs met and to do so without complaining. We were being trained to become a nation of scared, oppressed, sad, and hopeless souls despite our knowledge and unwilling adherence. At the time, it seemed that the oppressors were winning. Not conforming to their rules had serious consequences, for the guards were always present and they could arrest you, imprison you, and even kill you at will.

By this point, Dad was the cook in the house. After his imprisonment, he never actively searched for a new profession. Instead, he spent most of his time walking around town, working on his car, and trying out new recipes in the kitchen. He was mostly quiet and didn't talk much. His quiet and kind presence however gave me the peace I needed in the most turbulent part of my life. He gave me love and confidence all his life and never stopped even after the disgraceful ousting from the army. I loved him more than life. I still do.

The night the capital was attacked, I was 19 years old and had already finished high school couple of years prior. I had been a good student all my school life and, standing there in the little shelter in the basement, holding my father's hand as my mother cried nearby and our lives could end at any moment, it was hard not to think about where I should have been by now. I graduated high school with honors and was supposed to have an easy ride into the college of my choosing.

In Iran, it could be a very difficult path for high school graduates to get into any university. This was partly because of the lack of universities in our country, limiting the number of students they could take, and also the sheer number of applicants due to the lack of a good future or a decent income through available trade jobs. I, however, was ranked top of my co-graduates and was supposed to have an easier path to enter higher education and a professional position.

Unfortunately, my dreams of continuing onto college were crushed when the regime decided to close the universities in order to put in place a cultural and educational overhaul of the old system and turn these institutions into a country-wide Islamic educational system. They proclaimed the entire educational system needed to shut down before the completely new Islamic-oriented system could be put in place. The regime did not want to continue educating younger generations with the ways of the past or the principles of the Western civilization. There didn't seem to be any concern shown for how this decision would affect millions of the young population of the country. As the universities and colleges were shut down, nothing was offered to replace them. Then we finally realized the universities and colleges had been shut down indefinitely. My life was ruined. I had to come up with an entirely different plan for my life. Fast.

Once the universities were closed, all high school graduates, including myself, were expected to sign up for the army and consequently participate in the Iran/Iraq war. However, we also knew hundreds of thousands of young soldiers were being sent to the front lines to walk over the land mines installed by Iraqi Special Forces. Rather than putting money into training the new recruits, we were expected to simply march in and clean the mines out for revolutionary soldiers by sacrificing ourselves for Islam. We were promised doing so would turn us into martyrs. This war, like any other war, was senseless and non-apologetic. The younger generation was slowly being slaughtered at the front lines in the name of Islam and there was nothing anyone could do to stop them.

My only other choice was to live underground and be on the constant run from the revolutionary guards. If I were lucky, I'd be able to keep up this low profile and wait it out as long as I could. I picked this option. I'd been doing it for couple of years now with no end in sight.

There were whispers on the street though, of young people paying their way out of the country illegally and going to Europe or even Canada to apply for asylum.

"Once you get out, you can do anything," one friend whispered to me. "You can even go to college over there and live your life in peace."

The idea of getting the hell out of the abyss I was living in and going to school in another country where I was not being chased at all times sounded absolutely wonderful. I immediately started forming up a grand plan to somehow make enough money and pay my way out of the country by hiring a smuggler.

I kept my ears open and the plan began to take on greater shape and weight. I could cross the Iran border on the northwest corner, near where we had been attacked several years earlier, and I would enter Turkey. That would keep me safe from the revolutionary guards for a short time, but once in Turkey, I would have to find another smuggler to set me up with a fake Canadian visa and airline tickets. If I could get to Canada, I could declare asylum and start life over again. I hoped to get my foot into a university there and achieve my childhood dream of becoming an engineer. Eventually, I believed I would be able to bring my whole family to join me there and we could all live in peace, together, forever.

That was my plan. It was more like a dream and, at that point of my life, day-dreaming about my grand plan while listening to the BeeGees and Michael Jackson on my contraband Sony Walkman was all I had. I didn't have enough money or the necessary determination to go through such an undertaking, though. I could only play with the idea in my head and go over the details of the plan in my imagination while I stood in long lines to get my family's share of food or kerosene.

It took me some time, but I was finally able to purchase a fake ID and began work as a chemistry tutor for high school kids. I was the best student in my high school chemistry class and I even got promoted to chemistry lab supervisor for the last two years of my high school training. Teaching and tutoring high school level chemistry came so easy to me and it was good to feel productive again. I was making a decent amount of money at the same time, saving for my exodus. Living underground with a fake identity was difficult, making it impossible to fully relax at any time. It was not something I was planning to do for the rest of my life, but it was my first necessary step on the road to finding a way out of that situation.

I got to know many different people and their families while I was tutoring. I found my best friend through my tutoring endeavor. He, too, was tutoring and happened to live only a block down from my house. We shared a similar family history, since his father was also an ex-army colonel. He had lived with similar dreams of becoming an educated professional just to realize the luck of the draw placed him in a country where the government was against the western style of education we hoped for and there was no way out of the situation but to go underground and try to make a living.

Soon we became close friends and tried other ventures in business together. Within a couple of months of our meeting, we found an opportunity for a small manufacturing business. During the first several years after the Islamic revolution, most countries had put Iran under economic sanction and most of our industries were under pressure to produce necessary items rather than importing them. One of those necessary items under sanction which was not being imported was ladies' bras. As ordinary as it sounds, this was an essential item for the entire female population of the country. It was a consumable item and the whole importing industry was under an extreme shortage of bras. My friend's uncle was an importer in desperate need of essential parts for bras. The hooks and eyes, the under and side wires, and a few other items were of particular interest. We were commissioned by him to come up with a plan to produce all those parts with raw materials that could be resourced from within the country.

We had no clue where to look for all those items and certainly no experience with how they went together. But we were young and motivated. We both realized this could be the money-making opportunity we needed and my way out of the country. After many, many sleepless nights and a great deal of hard work, within the first year of operations we were able to locate all the raw material we needed. We designed and built the machinery to produce every single item necessary to finalize the production of several sizes of bra parts.

After the initial sales of more than three million sets of hooks and eyes, the business was booming. We had 8 employees working full time and a few part timers would join us from time to time. Money was coming in fast and my bank account was filling up quickly. Everything seemed to be working out fine. We both quit tutoring and spent most of our time managing the business. Life seemed to be easier and happier until that fateful summer night of bombing in Tehran.

The morning after the initial bombing, my family and I came out of the make shift shelter still shocked. We each silently went back to our rooms. No one was talking, and it seemed like all of us had received a beating to our souls. I could tell none of us had any hopes of the situation getting better anytime soon. After the night of bombing, I was ready to put my plan of two years into action. I had more than enough money and had enough of living in hiding and under constant danger and stress. Sitting on my bed that morning, I made up my mind.

My parents were sitting silently in the living room when I came out to talk with them. One look at their serious expressions as they saw me enter and I knew they could feel a shift in me. Once I brought up the idea of my plan, there was barely any resistance from any member of my family. My sister cried, and my brother just watched with big eyes, but no one argued.

My first step to convince my family that my plan made sense was an unexpectedly easy one. I thought any parent in their right mind would reject the idea of letting their 19-year-old kid to go through illegal border crossings for any reason, especially with all that cash and through a warzone. But the deteriorating conditions in Iran and especially the inevitable conclusion of my situation seemed much more dangerous to hold onto than my plan for escape. They even offered to help me in any way they could.

For the next five months, I went through a vigorous and careful process of finding a trustworthy smuggler and making preparations for the trip. I knew two of my high school friends had already made it to Canada and were accepted as migrants over there. They were already studying at the local colleges. Their father was a man on our block who knew my father. I contacted him and was able to track down the person who helped them get through the checkpoints and to the Turkish border. The smuggler was hesitant to do the job. There had recently been a mass of border crossers who had successfully passed over the hills on the Turkish border and the local revolutionary guards had put in place a number of increased security measures to ensure no one else escaped. However, the man couldn't resist helping me when he was offered a good amount of money to do the job.

After I paid his fees and planned the route and contacts I'd need along the way, I exchanged most of my money into foreign currency through underground exchange agents. I hid all of it in secret compartments in my clothes. To avoid arousing suspicion from the guards at the expected roadblocks, my parents planned to give me a ride to the nearest border town in northwestern Iran. If questioned by the guards, we were supposed to claim that we were going to my cousin's wedding. I even had a few invitations professionally printed with fake names and real addresses just to make sure we had convincing documents.

The plan was to meet with the team of smugglers in the suburbs of a city called Khoy in the northwest of Iran. After making that connection, I would walk with the smugglers through snow-covered backcountry roads all night toward the border and eventually cross the border into Turkey sometime around morning. On the other side of the border in Turkey, some villagers were paid to meet us with horses. From there, we would go to the nearest town and catch a train ride to Istanbul. There, another contact would meet me and arrange my trip to Canada, complete with a fake visa and a plane ticket. The rest of the plan was not particularly clear because it was difficult to make those connections from within Iran. I was confident I could competently play it by ear. Everything looked good on paper and it was supposedly tested at least twice with successful results. My friends already in Canada were proof of that. That was my awesome, infallible plan!

Chapter 2

The Attempt

I was looking out of the window of my room at the snow-covered streets of Tehran waiting for the guests to arrive. My parents had devised a party we could invite our friends to as a front for my actual going-away party. I was supposed to be happy and excited, yet I was feeling empty and blue, just like the cold and empty street of my city below. My teenage life so far was filled with horrible stories of violence, death and war, interspersed here and there with a few of the colorful and temporary moments of arbitrary excitement found in any teenager's life.

For example, my first real girlfriend was the sweet Jewish girl from a very prominent, affluent family who lived nearby. She was partly responsible for those short sparks of sweet moments in my teenage life. A soft kiss, her light-filled laughter, and the warm touch of her hand in mine were like bandages on the raw edges of my soul. Then one day, she simply disappeared along with her entire family. Years later, I found out they too, took the border route to escape persecution by government agents.

After her departure, I never pursued love and affection from another girl as long as I lived in Iran. What would be the point? I had no intention of staying longer than I could and everyone else was either looking to escape themselves or were working as eyes for the government. Most of my encounters with new people were that of a random and short-time relationship.

Standing in my window waiting for the guests to arrive, it seemed very hard to put a sweet and colorful tint on the pale and gray palette of my younger life. Yet, I was still very sad to leave.

My parents had invited family members and some of my friends for a celebration that had nothing to do with my leaving. Most of the guests didn't know anything about my plans and very few guests, including my best friend and business partner, were aware of what was supposed to happen the very next day. While other guests had smiles on their faces and were having fun, I couldn't help but notice the grim looks on my parents and my sister's faces. They knew I was going to dive onto an ocean of unknowns and dangerous undertakings within 12 hours.

That night, I couldn't sleep. I was both excited and sad at the same time, although I was not afraid. I felt ready to pull out and leave all those torturous days behind me. It was exciting to think about the adventure I was about to take, the first time I would be away from my family on my own. At the same time, it would be the first time I would be away from my family, on my own, and I had no idea how long it would be before I'd be able to see them again. Still, I was willing to take any risks available, no matter how dangerous they seemed to be, to get a chance at a better future on my own terms.

Early morning, while it was still dark in the sky, we were packed and ready to go. The streets were empty and filled with ice and snow. I said good-bye to my sister and little brother and blew them a kiss as they looked on from behind the window. I said good-bye words, but my heart wasn't ready to leave my home and my family behind. I turned my head around as my Dad started the car and took a deep breath. Was I ready to do this?

It was going to be a 12-hour trip to the border town where I was supposed to meet up with the smuggler. With the winter road conditions, we could be driving for even more hours. Exhausted but not yet at our destination, we arrived in the city of Tabriz after dark and decided to stay the night at a hotel even though we were only a few hours away from the border. It was a simple hotel in the outskirts of the town and seemed just the rest we needed before finally saying good-bye. The hotel was nothing fancy and it seemed to be a random choice. The perfect stop to spend a last night together.

It wouldn't take too long for us to figure out our stay in that hotel was just one of many mistakes we made in trying to get me out of the country. After dinner, I found a quiet corner in the lobby and lit a cigarette. I was trying to be respectful to my parents and did not smoke in front of them, yet my nerves were on edge. As I started the second one, I noticed most guests at the lobby eerily resembled us. There were a lot of parents with their 18- to 20-year-old kids. The parents all had emotionless facial expressions plastered on them, just like my parents. The kids all had that same excited but sad expression I'd noticed on my own face in the mirror. They were all worried but pretending to be cool. A friendly looking waiter was serving hot teas all around the lobby. He wore an ominous smile on his face, but his eyes did not take part in the smile. I couldn't take my eyes off of his menace look.

You're being paranoid again; I thought to myself.

Living most of my memorable life in the past several years in hiding and suspecting most everyone, it was easy to be paranoid about a strange looking and an extremely obliging fellow. But the question kept running through my super disorganized mind: Was this hotel really a random choice for everybody with the same plan? Was this place a natural choice for all "RUNNERS"? And if so, was this a bad thing that we were all here right now? Before my thoughts went too far down that trail, I felt a warm hand on my shoulder. It was my dad looking down at me with a smile.

"Did I scare you?" he asked, handing me a box of Marlboro Lights cigarettes. "You're going to need this," he added with a kind smirk.

He was right!

The next morning, we were back on the road along with several other vehicles from the hotel around us. We knew there were roadblocks set up before us, with the first one expected in a few miles. All three of us had practiced the same story in case the revolutionary guards stopped us. We came upon the first roadblock and one of the guards waved his flashlight at us in an obvious motion to tell us to slow down. As we approached, though, he seemed to change his mind and instead gave us the hand signal to go through. In the backseat, I could hear my heart pounding out of my chest. I was holding my breath. My hands were clammy and cold. I tried to avoid making eye contact with the guard as we slowly drove by him but caught the edge of a grin on his face. In surprise, I couldn't help but to look up. We locked eyes and his grin turned to a wide smile.

Thousands of bad thoughts rushed into my head in that instant. I had a very bad feeling building in the pit of my stomach. After my observations from last night, I was ready to call off the trip and ask my dad to turn around. But would that have drawn more suspicion? I stayed quiet and tried to make myself believe that the guard was probably just having a good day. I wasn't used to seeing any revolutionary guards with a happy face, though. Not ever. So, this was strange. Something was wrong. Something was seriously wrong.

Cold sweat took over my body. The whole situation seemed like a trap. My thoughts as well as my breathing stopped as I looked ahead. There was another roadblock only few hundred yards away and there was a little shack right next to it. There were several guards standing in the middle of the road. They were all looking directly at us as we slowly drove towards them.

My dad quickly turned his head around and with a low voice told me," Everything will be all right, Keep your cool. I won't let anything bad happen to you," as if he already knew everything was about to go wrong.

The guards signaled us to stop. None of them were smiling. Two guards came right at us, flanking the car. One of them opened my door.

"Step out of the car, please," he said as he opened the door. There was no hint of a request in his voice.

I looked at my dad as if I was asking his permission.

"There must be a mistake," my dad calmly told the guard. "We are simply on our way to a wedding …"

"Quiet!" Another guard yelled at him. "You will get out of the car, too!"

Once the two guards dragged my dad out of the car, I knew I had to go with them. I touched my mom's shoulder and she grabbed my hand. She was crying.

"I need to go with them, Mom," I said and got out of the car.

Getting out of the car I was still thinking about the first guard who let us pass through the check point. Suddenly, I remembered where I had seen that creepy smile before. He was the waiter from the night before at the hotel. He was the snitch. He was waiting patiently for all of us.

My entire blood pumped up to my head after the sudden realization. My eyes were on fire. It felt like I was woken up from a nightmare only to realize that the nightmare continues. One of the guards pushed me into the little shack next to the road. There were no windows and it seemed like a make-shift structure, metal sheets quickly latched together to create a little holding box, or maybe just to give the guards some shelter from the wind.

Without windows, the inside of the shack was dark, but some light was oozing through cracks around the door and other small gaps here and there. My hopeful thoughts that it was just a windbreak for guards were dashed when I noticed two more guards standing there with their automatic guns at the ready just watching me. I was frightened and visibly shaking, knowing I would be facing physical and mental abuse and possibly torture. Heck, I wasn't even sure I wouldn't just get shot. Everything was possible in the hands of revolutionary guards.

I only had a few seconds to make all these observations before the sudden, painful crack of a rifle heel struck the side of my face. My next clear impression was a close-up of the floor. The taste of my own blood filled my mouth and I heard nothing but a loud ringing in my head. The floor was wet and smelled like pee. I thought about my parents. This was entirely my fault. I dragged them into this. I was so selfish. A selfish 20-year-old. How did I not think up a better plan that didn't involve my parents? How could I have put my entire family at risk like this? What might be happening to my father and mother right now?

The guards told me to get up. Obediently, I began pulling my legs and arms into position to help me stand. I hadn't even gotten to my knees before the second wave of beating started. This time, it was hard boots coming from all sides. The men were swearing, spitting on my face, and kicking me all at the same time. Once they worked out their initial energy, it seemed it was time for questioning.

"You planned to cross the border illegally, didn't you?"

KICK!

"Who were you going to meet?"

KICK!

"You were going to help them overthrow the regime, weren't you?"

KICK!

"You are part of their espionage!"

The kicking and questioning continued as they tried to get me to confess to everything they could imagine. Little did they know my only plan was to get as far as I could away from war and politics and just go to school. What a basic need yet so hard to get. But did they care? Would they have believed me if I had a chance to tell them?

At some point, I found myself flat on my back in the box. Half my face was swollen, and blood was oozing out of my mouth when I realized the beating had stopped. Instead, they were pulling my clothes off me and ripping them apart. They knew I had all my money hidden in various parts of my clothes. How did they know that?

As I watched my life and everything in it being torn apart literally in front of my eyes, the noises around me became muffled and everything seemed to happen in slow motion. I didn't hear them as much as see them laughing as they pulled every dollar bill out of my not-so-hidden compartments. Bills were flying around and falling on the ground as the soldiers scrambled to grab more. They were salivating over the find, over their victory.

Victory? Ahh, how many days, how many months did I work to make that money? How often had I fantasized about going to a university and living a normal life? I felt the warm streak of a tear on my cheek as my complete defeat hit me. The sense of losing all I had was unbearable. All I'd worked for and all my plans and wishes, possibly, probably, even my entire family had been drawn into this with me. I took a deep breath, closed my eyes, and wished to die. The best I could hope for now was a swift, quiet death.

Only after the soldiers ensured they'd collected every scrap of money from under or around my nude form did they throw a khaki-colored dirty jumpsuit at me.

"Put that on," one of them ordered.

I did my best to get dressed after the beating and the humiliation of being stripped, but I was not fast enough for them. One of them impatiently pulled the collar up and around my neck while another roughly handcuffed my hands behind my back. A third dropped a dirty, smelly, uncomfortably moist black hood over my head. At that moment, I was almost sure they were going to kill me. I wondered why they bothered to make sure I was dressed first.

They pushed me to my knees on the damp floor and I could hear them moving all around me, gathering to one side of the shack. I tried not to cry or make any noise. I tried not to plead for my life. What was really left of it anyway? A loud bang echoed through the room, causing me to jump on my knees and then crumple to the ground as I realized the sound had been nothing more than the guards slamming the door of the shack behind them as they'd exited. The smell of urine had grown stronger in the shack and I hoped it was because my nose was now closer to the floor rather than I'd wet myself. Given my current conditions, it was almost impossible for me to tell the difference.

As far as I could tell, they'd left me alone inside the box. I could hear muffled noise coming from outside and an occasional burst of laughter. Slowly, painfully, clumsily, I managed to prop myself up and moved to a sitting position against one of the walls. I couldn't stop thinking about my parents. I knew my dad was in big trouble since he was an ex-army colonel from the previous regime. With his arrests and everything, I knew he had all kinds of negative elements going for him. And now, they had a sweet deal; they also had his son in their custody as a "fugitive".

Within an hour, someone came in the box and pulled me to my feet. I felt the straight stock of a rifle across my back as he silently pushed me forward until I could feel the warmth of the sun on my shoulders and a cold breeze tugged at the black hood around my head. It was hard to move forward without knowing where I was going, and I kept stumbling, not wanting to move too much farther ahead than I could feel. Eventually, I realized I was expected to climb up into the open bed of a truck. It was toward the end of winter, but the northwestern provinces are known for their horrible cold winters. I could feel the truck shaking after I was settled, but I couldn't tell if they were loading other prisoners, other soldiers, or just getting on and off. To be safe, I remained silent. Once the truck started driving, the cold air seeped into my borrowed jumpsuit and numbed my entire body. I was oddly grateful for the hood on my head because at least it helped to keep my face from freezing.

After about 20-minutes, we arrived at our destination. Later, I found out it was the revolutionary guard's prison created specifically for people like me who attempted to flee the country.

"Get down!" a voice ordered gruffly.

I wasn't sure whether it was directed at me or someone else, but the question was answered when someone tugged firmly on my collar. I had to move my frozen feet fast to keep from landing face-first on the ground behind the truck. It felt like my feet hit the ground and only stumbled a few steps when someone new was forcing me to drop to my knees with a slap to the back of my legs.

Everyone was speaking angrily. I wondered whether they were really angry or if this was just part of the intimidation strategy. Wasn't this their job to deal with people like us? Wasn't I what they expected to deal with that day? Maybe it was part of the whole thing to sound and seem scary. Whatever the answer, they were doing a great job at scaring me.

After a while, the angry discussion amongst them ended and it seemed they were no longer interested in me. I remained still on my knees, in the middle of where, I still had no idea though it felt somehow inside. It wasn't concrete or gravel under my knees. No one was asking me questions or kicking me around. I couldn't hear anyone close and that gave me a small bit of courage. I took the opportunity to use my tongue to try to move the black cloth off of my head. I managed to move it just enough to peek out from under the bag. I could see about two feet away from me along the ground, confirming I was kneeling on a finished floor. That was not enough to give me the information I wanted, though. I had to see where I was and make some guesses about what was going to happen to me. I started struggling to get the cloth off my head. In doing so, I moved around a little more and felt the heat of a radiator on the wall to my side. I used the knob on the radiator to get the hood away from my face. Now I could see that I was sitting in a narrow hallway with no doors. Directly across from me on the other wall was another hot water radiator. Now that I thought about it, I realized I'd been slowly warming from the heat on my frozen knees.

As I got warmer, the handcuffs started to hurt and my knees started to protest, but that was the least of my concerns. After a while I heard a commotion and a bunch of people entered the hallway. In the middle of them, they led my dad, blindfolded and handcuffed. They were so excited about arresting my father, they didn't even notice the cloth pulled away from my face. Just like a bunch of coyotes finding a bigger and juicier prey, they were drooling around the now helpless ex-officer of Shah's army.

I could hear my dad breathing hard as they chained him to the other radiator. I wondered what they'd done to him in the time since I'd last seen him. Had he gone through a similar 'questioning' process I'd experienced in the shack? But once the crowd left, Dad just sat there, looking almost as lost and alone as I'd felt. What was going through his mind? I was furious. My eyes were burning from anger. He did not deserve this. He was the nicest man I knew. Why would anyone do this to him?

I whispered, "I'm here, Dad. I'm all right, I'm all right, Dad."

He looked up and smiled gently. "I'll fix this soon. I promise," he said quietly.

Sounds of men approaching again reached us. This time they were coming for me. They didn't seem pleased about my hood being off, but they didn't make a big deal of it either as they led me down the hallway toward the interior of the building. After that brief encounter, I didn't see my dad for another ten months.

From the hallway, I was taken to a semi-dark and damp solitary cell. It didn't take me long to measure it off as a six-foot by four-foot room surrounded by unusually tall walls, maybe 10-12 feet high. There was a small opening very close to the ceiling where the cold outside air seeped in. Scared, cold and hungry, I tried to focus on anything positive, or anything other than the present situation. More than anything, I was disappointed at myself for having tried such a poorly planned and executed endeavor. My head was spinning, and my mind kept replaying through each step we took. With hindsight, each step from the beginning stood out as a huge mistake. I had no one but myself to blame. I shouldn't have listened to the smuggler. I should have trusted my instincts and common sense.

Why didn't I take the dirt road to bypass the roadblock? Why did I bring all my money with me instead of transferring it through other channels? Why did I choose to approach the border during the daylight? Why did I choose to go through this during the coldest winter? Why did I let my parents get involved? What would happen to my brother and sister now? The questions and self-recrimination never stopped.

"Follow me, you son of a bitch," the guard yelled while kicking the door open some hours, days, or weeks later.

The first thought that ran through my head was a terror-filled moment of where is he taking me? It didn't seem reasonable to think they would be letting me free so soon. I worried again that they were going to kill me. They could.

There was nothing to stop them. One less army brat trying to get out of the country. I wondered if they would let my parents know of my execution. I hoped they wouldn't tell them. What an end for such a promising student, Random and useless like a bad movie. My wandering thoughts came to an immediate halt and my heart started pounding painfully when I saw a few more guards shifting outside the door, each holding automatic rifles.

The first guard immediately hand-cuffed me again and covered my head with what I was pretty sure was the same smelly bag I'd had on earlier. He started pushing me forward toward where I knew the opening of the cell was. We turned, I heard a door opening and then I felt the breeze and cold air letting me know we had somehow already reached the outdoors again.

"Get on your knees," my guard ordered as he pushed me down. My knees sank in slushy snow.

"Are you going to get rid of me?" I practically whispered, half afraid to ask, half afraid not to ask.

The guard gave me no answers other than to laugh loudly and stomp away, leaving me still kneeling, blind and helpless in the snow. It seemed like I was kneeling there for a long time. Snow was melting around my knees and the ice water was seeping through my flimsy pants. Questions of what they were going to do with me continued to run through my mind. I couldn't breathe. My head was spinning and my heart was hammering against my ribs. I was scared. But I felt that I was ready. I was ready to end this.

"I'm ready, I'm ready," I whispered over and over.

I heard footsteps crunching in the snow and approaching very slowly. As they got close, I felt someone's hand on my face over the bag, feeling the contours as if he were blind. Through the bag he pushed two fingers into my nostrils and started pulling me forward.

I fell in the snow with my face, my legs long since numb in the snow.

He yelled, "Who were you going to join on the other side? When were you going to come back? Give all of their names or I will kill you right now, I swear I'll kill you right now and I will enjoy doing it."

I had no satisfying answer for him. This type of questioning became my hour-long routine for the next three months. If I wasn't in the yard waiting for someone to shoot me, I was in my solitary cell in the revolutionary guard's prison. They usually took me to the back yard in the snow and kicked me around or pulled me by my nose while my face was covered and my hands cuffed. They asked me about my dad and my schoolmates. They threatened to kill me almost every day. After a few days, I knew the routine and after a week, I was not afraid anymore. I was just angry.

I was allowed to use the restroom twice a day and shower once a week. I had to have my head covered every time I left my cell. I had to wake up very early in the morning for prayer in my cell. Food was pushed through a small opening under the cell's metal door. They gave me bread for breakfast, cheese and bread for lunch and more bread for dinner. I had a large water container that I could fill up every time I used the bathroom. But mostly, solitary was just that, solitary. For many hours a day, I was in the small damp and dim cell by myself. Sometimes, when I couldn't take it anymore and the sound of silence was deafening, I would just lie on my back and look up into the dark ceiling. I would feel that I was melting into its darkness and, for a brief moment, I was safe and warm.

While solitary was scary, depressing and all and all horrible, it affected me and my character in some positive ways as well. When all my dreams and plans came crashing down on the day I was arrested, I thought I had nothing left to live for and I'd much rather die. Solitary pushed me to think my whole life with a new perspective. I learned to be patient, very patient. I learned to count my blessings and not take ordinary things for granted. Daily beatings and tortures only made me feel stronger. Those monsters turned me into a different person. One that I liked. A stronger one. One that could kick out and tame all the demons in my head. While I didn't realize it at the time, solitary also made me ready to move into a regular prison and join the general prison population. One spring day, someone opened the door and told me to follow them. This time, I really was leaving.

No head cover was required this time, and no one was yelling, immediately marking this trip as something different. I was hand-cuffed and directed through a narrow corridor into a bigger hall. I recognized the smells and even recognized the number of steps it took to cross the space and the direction we took to reach it, but this was the first time I was actually seeing where we were going. It was a strange feeling to be able to see something for the first time that I was already so familiar with. It was also strange to realize I was enjoying my ability just to see it.

The soldiers asked me very politely to go through the exit door and jump in the back of a truck. Their politeness was puzzling. I worried this was perhaps some new kind of trap. Maybe they knew by now that I was just a regular person with no affiliation to political and anti-revolutionary groups. Whatever it was, I welcomed the change, decided to enjoy the moment, and allowed myself to feel more like a human again.

Riding in the back of the truck was also a weird feeling. Try not riding in a car for a few months and you'll understand how I felt. It was springtime by then, and the cool northwestern air was filling my lungs. After months of solitary in mostly stifling confinement, any freedom was a celebration for my body and soul. I was mesmerized by the random sights of trees, streets, and people. My face was covered mostly by the long beard I'd grown while in prison the past three months, however I could still feel the warm tears on my cheeks. I had endured solitary and torture. Under that thick skin and pile of facial hair I'd developed, I was still alive.

Chapter 3

The Prison

The guards and I arrived at the old wooden gates of the county prison before noon. The doors of the prison were opened just long enough to let us inside a medium-sized inner exercise yard. There were no prisoners in the yard when we entered, but I could hear enough noises coming from a hallway not far from where we were, letting me know the prison was occupied. The brick-covered open space was covered with moss, but the smell of bleach was overpowering. I held a brief hope that perhaps this prison would be more sanitary than the last one. A revolutionary guard jumped from the cab of the truck and pulled me down from the back. Without giving me time to settle my feet, he pushed me toward a nearby prison guard.

"Here is your fucking gift for today. His father was a colonel in Shah's regime," my guard said with a nasty smile in my direction. "All yours now," he added as he turned away and climbed back into the cab of the truck.

The prison guard seemed to be different somehow from the revolutionary guard member. He was wearing a different-looking uniform, for one thing. But he also didn't have the same look of utter disgust on his face that most of my guards had had so far. I assumed it was because I was at the county prison, but I wasn't sure.

"Where am I?" I meekly asked the prison guard.

"Shut up!" he yelled angrily.

As he slammed me face-first into the wall behind us, I quickly realized I was not in a better situation by any means.

Fortunately, his only purpose was to take my handcuffs off. As I rubbed feeling back into my fingers, he pushed me through another set of doors where I met my prison-mates for the first time. There weren't exactly cells per se in the prison. Based on what I could see, the whole structure was probably built at the turn of the 20th century. The prison was made up of several huge rooms with concrete floors covered by old rags and fronted by bars. There was no furniture in any of the cells and each room was scattered with prisoners' belongings. Narrow hallways connected the rooms and led to another yard. As we entered this second yard, I could see a volleyball court and a series of toilets on the other side. The only privacy the 'facilities' offered were doors cut in half. Guards had to monitor prisoners even while they were using the bathroom! There were also some faucets sticking out of the wall where prisoners washed up and brushed their teeth. The walls were whitewashed and stood about 25 feet tall. On all four corners of the yard, there were posts where guards took turns watching the prisoners.

I was taken to the farthest room on the day of my arrival. The other prisoners welcomed me by whistling and shouting profanity as I was marched past the other cells and pushed into my own. It didn't bother me. I had my ears full of that in the last few months during the torture sessions. There were a few window casings high above which held nothing but broken glass overlooking the "play yard". It was awkward standing there in the middle of the cell, surrounded by a variety of men who, I later learned, could have committed any type of crime. Prisoners weren't separated here by order of offense, but rather just grouped within cells based on which ones had the most room at the moment. We stared at each other for about 10 minutes before another guard came in and blew his whistle. Every man in the cell scrambled into a line. Most of them were holding some form of dish or container. It was lunchtime.

I hesitated, not sure what was expected of me.

The guard looked at me and yelled, "Get in the line, faggot."

I joined the others already in line. Something tapped me lightly on the shoulder. At the same time, I heard a voice near the back of my head.

"Don't turn back. I have an extra dish. You can use it until you buy your own."

The man behind me slowly extended his hand forward. He was holding an old and badly stained plastic bowl.

"Take it. Take it quick"

Through quick whispers and rumors, I learned his name was Saeed and he was serving a 20-year prison term for assault and robbery. He was the presumed leader of the

Kurdish non-lifers within the prison population. Soon, I learned that the prison inmate system was made up of a complicated hierarchy. Just like a military compound, the hierarchy system was enforced meticulously. Anyone and everyone had earned their place in the hierarchy through a complicated mix of random and organized procedures.

After dinner, we were herded back into our communal cells. Since I didn't yet have a place within the hierarchy system, I spent a miserable night shoved against the bars at the front of the cell, one of the least desirable spaces available.

Early the next morning, the guards dragged me back out of the cell and out to the second courtyard. Without explaining what they were doing, they forced my head under one of the faucets and proceeded to shave my head. In keeping with Islamic tradition, they did not shave my beard. After all the beatings I'd been given over the past three months, once my head was shaved and all those injuries were made visible, I looked like a tough guy. It wasn't that I had a mirror to look into, but I could see the expressions of horror, shock, and respect that came over the men's eyes when I was led back to my cell. Maybe that's why I was almost instantly promoted to the presumed leader of a group of prisoners called "The Crossers". There were 18 kids, my age or younger, who were imprisoned for the same reason I was. Our crime was having attempted an unauthorized border crossing. None of us actually committed a real crime other than wanting to leave but nevertheless, we were captured, tortured and now imprisoned. Once every day, the faction leaders of the prison would sit down and, over a hot tea and lots of cigarette smoking, decide how we wanted to divide the prisoner's tasks for the day.

Incarceration changes people in ways that were unimaginable to me before I spent months amongst prisoners of all types. Most prisoners were turned into the worst version of themselves possible. Some discovered their human side and became totally rehabilitated. For me, it was to learn what I had always lacked throughout my younger life; patience and endurance. Before I got myself and my father arrested on that cold, winter day while on the road to freedom, I had almost no patience to put up with the slightest changes in my life that were not going according to my plans. As a teenager, probably just like most teenagers, I imagined the whole world revolved around me and anything that interfered with my plans was operating in a personal affront against me.

In prison, however, nothing went according to my plans. Every day could bring a new rule, increased limitations, new rights, or unforeseen challenges. One had to have an enormous amount of patience and endurance to be able to go through months of solitary and months of dirty and crowded prison rooms and still come out the other side with some sanity.

I didn't.

Once they learned where I was, my mom took a 12-hour bus ride every Thursday night. She'd arrive around noon on Friday in Khoy, just in time for visiting hours. We'd talk as long as we could, then she'd wait at the bus station for the next bus home, riding another 12 hours back. She did that for many months, 24 hours of round-trip bus ride every week in order to get seven minutes of visiting time with her son in prison. Her visits kept me going. Of course, being able to talk with her for a few minutes each week made me feel better and stay in touch with things that were happening back at home. Plus, she would bring me food items, money, cigarettes, and most of all, a few sets of new underwear! Some things I would use myself while others I could trade with the other prisoners for favors such as a better sleeping spot or to get out of a task I didn't want to do.

All prisoners slept on the floor. Apparently, the prison felt furniture could be turned into weapons too easily and we were not allowed to have mattresses. Prisoners were allowed a space of 1.5 x 6 feet to sleep at night. The prison was so overcrowded that sometimes even that much room was not available. Every night I spent at that prison, I had to sleep on my shoulder to one side. There was no other way to fit within the space we were allowed. It was very uncomfortable and even painful at first but, in time, like everyone else in the cells, I got used to it. My best dreams were about being able to lay on a bed, stretch out my arms, and sleep on my back. I wondered if I'd ever get the chance to sleep like that again.

For a variety of reasons, lice were prominent throughout the entire prison environment. While most people tend to think of head lice when they hear the term, these were body lice. They were only attracted to the stitches and folds on clothing items. Remember, our only 'bedding' was the pile of overlapping rags that had been thrown over the concrete. My first few weeks at the prison were like a torture chamber of its own. I was constantly battling the lice attack, itching all over, and kept trying to shake them off my clothes. It didn't take too long before I decided resistance was futile. Just like everybody else, I gave in and the vermin infested all my clothing.

Food in the prison was not edible. I don't mean not edible in the sense that it was my most hated vegetable every night. Even the inmate old timers found it difficult to get past its horrible smell and taste. Every meal turned my stomach as I wondered just what we might be eating exactly. On my second lunch in the prison, they handed out a spoonful of grey juice with some unidentified solid pieces of something floating in it.

The person in front of me inspected his plate and, with the big smile of a fisherman after catching a big one, turned to me and said, "Here is the tail! You might get the body in your dish."

He dangled a cooked mouse-tail in front of my face.

My anxiety and the lingering emotional and physical pain of my tortures turned into heartache and hopelessness as the days passed. Spending my days in the prison, counting the hours but not knowing what was going to happen to me or when things might change was dreadful. Pacing all day by the tall, dirty walls of the prison yard turned me into a sad and restless caveman. For the first few weeks of imprisonment, I was happy and excited to see my mom through the wire mesh at the visiting room, but in time that excitement died as well, and I lost track of the days of the week.

Being deeply depressed for a long period of time alters one's state of mind. And it altered mine as well. Sadness turned into anger and hopelessness evolved into a brutal, vengeful state of mind. Reality seemed to take a twist through a dark mirror and I had a hard time seeing the actions I'd taken to mess up my own life. Instead, it was all too easy to blame the world around me. Emotionally, I became a time bomb ready to explode.

I blame this state of mind for the rampage I went on one night when they sent in a couple dozen new prisoners for our cell. I had just gotten to sleep when I was jolted awake by the guards' noisy entrance.

"Open some space for fresh meat, faggots."

The guards pushed the newcomers inside our holding room, a double line of men shuffling through the door.

"Get up losers. Open some space."

We were already piled on top of each other as it was. There were just too many prisoners for us to claim our full 1.5 x 6 foot space. After half an hour of wrangling, I'd finally claimed enough room to lay curled on my shoulder without being on top of or underneath someone else. Now they were trying to build us three deep? I was not going to lose my little space for nothing. The room seemed to take on a red tint as I jumped up from my sleeping position. I attacked the very first new-comer to come within my reach, pushing him out of the room.

"Get them the fuck out of here, you assholes," I yelled at the guards. "Don't you see we have no room? Get them the fuck out of here, you mother fuckers."

I felt the sharp pain of the first baton on my face, and it was enough to shut me up but not enough to keep others from striking. The second and third swipes came at my face while I was protecting it with my hands. I could hear the bones in my fingers cracking.

One week of solitary confinement was nothing for me. After all, I spent the first couple of months of my imprisonment in solitary confinement in the revolutionary guards' prison. In a way, I even enjoyed my time alone, uncrowded by the other prisoners, and able to sleep. But my face was swollen at a painful angle and I could only see through one eye. Both my pinkies were badly broken and swollen. Without any hope I would get medical attention any time soon, I did my uneducated best to straighten out the bones myself, but I could feel my pulse throbbing in my hands and face. By the end of the week when I was released from solitary, the pain and distension on my face had subsided, but my hands were in bad shape.

Once I got settled back into the general prison population, my only friend in jail, Saeed, mixed some eggs in a bowl with lots of cigarette ash. He cut my undershirt into long bands and submersed them into the beaten egg and ash mixture. He then wrapped my fingers and hands carefully with the gray egg-soaked bands. The bands dried in a few hours and created a makeshift cast. It was effective at keeping my hands and fingers straight as long as I kept them dry. For two weeks, I had those casts on my hands and depended on Saeed and my position as a faction leader to avoid getting into further trouble. To this day, especially when I type, my crooked and semi-disabled pinkies remind me of those days.

Several months passed and every day looked bleaker and more hopeless than the last. The guards never took me to a courtroom where I could receive a sentencing. They also refused to tell me how long I was going to be held at the prison. Some younger guys who were arrested for the same 'crime' I was being held for, attempting to cross the border, came and left within a few months. But I was still there, day after day, week after week, month after month. As far as I knew, they had thrown me in the prison and forgotten my existence.

Saturdays were the days when they called prisoner numbers. Over a loudspeaker, they would instruct inmates to pack their bags and go to the front. Usually, that meant those prisoners were being freed. No one was ever told ahead of time when they might be released, though they usually knew when it was getting close to the end of their sentence. Truthfully, no one had any idea what really happened to people once they left those doors, but if they were being transferred to another prison, there would be a truck in the first yard waiting to transport them and it wasn't ever done on a Saturday.

Many Saturdays I sat by the big gray metal door waiting to hear my number. But week after week, no one was calling me forward. Gradually, I came to hate Saturdays and moved as far as I could from that damn grey door.

It was a Wednesday morning when my usual activity of meeting with the other faction leaders was interrupted by the loud speakers.

"Inmate 8642, report to the front."

"Why are they calling my number?" I asked Saeed, leader of the non-lifers.

"It is not Saturday," he pointed out, a serious expression on his face.

I quickly replayed recent activities in my head. I hadn't done anything unusual that should have gotten me into trouble again.

“No engines,” the leader of the lifers pointed out, meaning there wasn’t a truck in the front yard waiting to transport me to another living hell.

“Maybe someone snitched on you,” Saeed said, with a suspicious glance around the yard.

Before the guards could get too excited about my non-compliance, I got up from our circle and headed toward the front. Once I got to the grey door, a guard stood in front of me with a bitter smile on his face.

“Get your shit and get the fuck out of here,” he said. “One less maggot for us to watch.”

Just like that, my nightmare seemed to be over.

Chapter 4

The Twilight Zone

It was a calm autumn morning when I walked through the series of gray metal doors into the old, damp brick yard for the last time. Just as the inmate leaders had suggested from within, there were no trucks in the yard waiting to take me away. I was completely clear of the doorway before I realized I'd been holding my breath, waiting for a guard to snap a hood over my head and the backs of my legs to be struck forcing me to fall on my knees on the brick. I'd been in prison for the better part of a year. It was hard not to think of this as some sort of new trick or torment they'd devised.

On my own, I passed through a guarded rusty metal double-door gate. It felt surreal, as if I was walking on another planet, somewhere far, far away from Earth and the wars we were fighting. Finally, I was out on the street. I was once again free.

No one was waiting for me outside the prison, but that didn't even occur to me at the time. I was so consumed by taking in everything around me on that random street that I didn't even realize, at first, I was there by myself. I was mesmerized looking at the trees and falling leaves. Everything appeared to me with an amazing depth and color. It seemed like I was high on the simple sense of freedom. I wasn't sure if that was possible, but I had never experienced anything like this in the past. After months of looking at cement walls, barbed wire, and chain links, anything with soft edges and color was amazing.

Within an hour, my parents, who were notified of the day but not the time of my release, showed up to take me home. They had stayed overnight at the house of a family member who lived in Tabriz, the largest city close to the prison in Khoy. Since my dad had lost our car during the arrest last winter, this family member was giving us all a ride. My mom was crying and laughing all at once all the way from the prison to Tabriz. And my dad had my hand in his. Even while I marveled at the movement we were making across the landscape so full of color and depth, I could sense the feeling of reassurance he felt simply by having my hand in his. He finally had me next to him where I was once again safe.

For myself, I was so overwhelmed by the weird and lovely feeling of moving in a car that I couldn't demonstrate the depth of my happiness about being freed and reunited with my family. Just sitting there on the cushioned seat, with the air at a comfortable temperature, able to move my hands and feet and all while moving at high speeds down the roadway was a lot like riding in a roller coaster for the very first time. Somewhere on the line between exciting and frightening, knowing what's happening and not having control of it, feeling safe and yet knowing there is a risk. It is an amazing sensory overload when all your normal life routines are interrupted and withdrawn for a long period of time, and then you are suddenly reintroduced to everything at once. That day was one of the best days of my very young life.

That night back at the family member's home in Tabriz, I laid down on the bed, the real bed, that stood in a guest room I had all to myself. I'd had a long bath in their never before used bathtub, where I was able to soak the infestation of lice away from my skin, I was wearing all new clothes my mother brought for me, and there was no threat of violence coming from any direction. I was free! I felt my whole body stretching as much as it could in every possible direction and I was enjoying every second of it. Months of sleeping on one shoulder had my muscles trained to be tight and motionless through the night. It hadn't really occurred to me how much that had interfered with my sleep while I was in prison. There were so many other things to be concerned about. Now, ahhh, I could move, sleep on my back, stomach, or just turn on my shoulder if I wanted to. I thought it might be difficult to sleep in strange surroundings, but I slept the peaceful and full sleep of a coma patient that night.

Prison, as much as I hated every second of it, was an education for my character and soul. It taught me humility, patience, and the ability to not take anything for granted, especially those little things that make life so comfortable like bug-free pillows and warm, fluffy blankets.

The next day, my parents and I got on a bus going back to Tehran and, before nightfall that evening, I found myself looking up at the same window through which I'd waved goodbye to my brother and sister so many months ago. There were hugs and kisses and laughter and tears for a while before everyone settled down and reality kicked in for me. I was really free and at home, but there was some challenges to face. The government freed me on one condition. I had to voluntarily sign up for the war and join the military. Otherwise, I was not allowed to work, continue my education or, of course, get out of the country. I was back at square one with far less money than the day I started this endeavor many months before!

Adding to my depression, I learned that while I was locked up, the universities were reopened and were offering much the same sort of education they'd offered before, with some major and minor field-specific alterations. Despite my relatively stellar performance as a student, though, I was not allowed to participate in the entrance examinations since I now had a prison record and had not gone through the two-year required military service. It was absurdly frustrating for me since the government was responsible for the closures in the first place, back when I was eligible and more than able to gain admission to my dreams. Now, through a series of unfortunate events, I was no longer qualified to do what I felt I could do best.

This felt like the twilight zone. I did not belong anywhere in our society unless I joined the military and participated in the war.

I had to do something with my life and it wasn't going to be military service. But, just like before, I knew I couldn't hide forever. At the very least, I had to help my family and I had to devise a new way to escape. I decided to start another business with my friends and hide under their identity. I would just work and save money for a while until I could come up with a good plan to flee the country and follow my dreams elsewhere.

After many meetings to explore ideas and extensive market research, we decided to open a French-style coffee shop. Thankfully, I still had some money left from my previous business and, with the help of my friends and now business partners, we leased a place in a more affluent part of the city. It didn't take us long to create a sharp-looking coffee shop, a very cool place for younger patrons to hang out, exactly the market we were targeting.

Looking back, I know I should have been pleasantly surprised by the strong survival instinct that had kept my mind and soul together through all of this. I had survived despite all odds against my family and me. I had survived despite the monsters that had haunted me throughout my childhood years. I was kicked down and pummeled to the ground by the government so many times, yet here I was, starting a whole new life, again. This was my second successful business venture, both started and operated as an illegal citizen in my own country, yet I was only 21. It should have been a matter of pride and accomplishment, but it never felt like that at all. I was still living under the shadow of my nightmares.

I had started my young life as a not-so-normal teenager with all kinds of demons in my head. I had led a life of terrifying turbulences and misfortunes. After prison, I really wanted to think that I am a better, stronger and more determined person by measuring my progress on financial and social success. In reality, however, I was horribly depressed and lonely inside. I tried hard to hide that from my family and friends. Although I had gone through and survived the most horrible years of my young life, but what I gained from all those torturous days, were deep scars and new collection of fears and anxieties in my soul and nightmares to keep me company every night. I would carry the pain through my entire adult life.

I had however, some bright spots in my daily life. I was almost happy spending time with my friends at the coffee shop. Taking care of our customers was always satisfying and I appreciated the gleaming clean surfaces and comforting smells of the shop. Most of the customers were in my age group, some a little older, some a little younger, many of them going to school. We could relate to each other as a peer group either lamenting the lack of options we'd had or living vicariously through the experiences of those who made it to college. It was a place where young people felt comfortable freely discussing our common problems and dilemmas. I made several new friends at the coffee shop and life seemed to settle into its normal place again. Things were going well until the day they found me.

Less than nine months after we opened the coffee shop, I was again arrested by the government's revolutionary police. They immediately took me to an army recruiting center's temporary holding cell. It turned out the revolutionary police had developed infiltrators whose jobs were to mingle amongst college students to spot people like me, who were avoiding the military, or anyone else who might be politically or religiously opposed to the regime in any way. Again, it was my own fault I was caught. I shouldn't have been so trusting in such a public environment and been so forthcoming to all and any friendly faces. For the next few years, I would be paying for my own sloppiness and stupidity. Or maybe, it was my destiny to end up that rainy spring day in the military holding cell.

I was kept overnight inside the holding cell. The next day, I was taken directly to the military preparation and distribution center in the middle of the city. It was a huge stadium filled with young guys like me who were mostly in attendance against their will. Our country was in the middle of a nonsensical and unjust war with Iraq. We heard the news about thousands upon thousands of young soldiers dying every day, and even more thousands were coming back on stretchers with their limbs blown off or burned into unrecognizable shapes.

I could see the desperation on most of the young faces around me as they looked at the reality of a terrifying future in an unconventional war. Most of the guys around me, and most of the guys in the stretchers coming home, did not support the government and its justification of war, but the army police brought them all here and gave them no options. There was no way out and no return. Strangely, I felt that I was relieved. As if I was waiting for them to capture me and take me where they wanted me to be. I just wanted for that feeling of horrible anticipation to be over. Yes, I was relieved.

We were ordered to make up lines of 100 people per line. I felt like I had no control over my body movements. I did not feel anything anymore, emotionally or physically. I came to realize I was simply an empty shell, one that could apparently move, robot-like, on external command. Once again, I was pushed, along with many others like me, in a direction which I never planned for or wanted to have any part in. The government had made the decision for us and we were carried forward as on a huge wave into a brutal war with dismal hope of surviving.

Lines were made, and I could hear all the nervous breathing around me. Rain was falling hard, and it was hard for me to keep my head up. I looked down and focused on a puddle forming at my feet. I felt in peace with my life. Rain had always had that effect on me. I mentally reviewed everything that had happened in the last few years in my life that brought me to here. Raindrops were trouncing my face and moving me back and forth between the reality and my thoughts. No matter how hard I worked to rise above, I continued to be beaten down and thrown into chaos. It was a never-ending battle that I was constantly losing. Losing was what I was really good at. Indifference settled over my heart and soul. I realized I truly had no purpose. It seemed like all my plans, hopes, and dreams were just that, pipe dreams. So why not join the war? That dark, cold, murky puddle was my life.

The men within the stadium, myself included, were divided into smaller groups, usually created by the simple luck of which line we ended up in. My group was selected to serve in the Navy. Suddenly, our entire groups chance of surviving the two-year military service increased by ten folds.

We were sent to training within two weeks after that melancholy rainy day of registration and selection. Those two weeks were filled with daily chores to take care of my business and remaining social life. Last few days was about saying good byes to family and friends. I couldn't imagine 'training' elsewhere would be any different, but three months in the southern desert of Iran near a town called Seerjan proved me wrong. Finally, I was transferred to an emergency medical unit as an ambulance driver for Naval Academy students. I spent the next 21 months with that unit, learning more than I thought I could, just driving a truck.

Chapter 5

Second Attempt

In After two years of military service, I was lucky enough to survive the war without any additional injuries beyond what I'd suffered in prison. I was two years older and it seemed like that I was much wiser than my years. I had learned to be patient and I was slimmer and fitter than I'd been as a teenager. I was now in my early 20's and considered myself to be an actual adult as compared to the boy I'd been just a few years ago. Although the entire two years of my military service was a constant challenge given the history of my family and my previous prison record, I always believed I could survive the dark energy surrounding me. Like the hero of every storybook, I faced the demons of my past around every turn. At no point during my service did someone ever let me forget I was, at one time, a deserter because I'd tried so hard to avoid military service. Wherever I went and no matter how hard I worked, I felt hostile eyes on me, as if I would run the first second I had a chance. With my minimum two years successfully served, though, I was finally released in good standing. Now that I had served my required time, I was even considered legal with no debt to the government. Free again! All and all, I felt better about myself and very hopeful about the future. Finally, I had the flexibility to move more as I wished.

Of course, my parents were fully aware of my decision to leave the country as soon as I finished my service in the military. They had survived all the hardship of my earlier escape attempt and the almost year I spent in prison and they did not want to endure another frightening adventure, but they were supportive of my decision and always turned their reassuring and smiling faces to me. Our country was still at war and I think my parents were hoping perhaps I could find a better way for both myself and for my younger brother when he finally became of age. He didn't want to go to war any more than I had, and no one could tell how long this conflict might last. At least this way, he'd have more options than what I'd faced.

Looking back, I know I did not fully appreciate or understand the degree of my parents' sacrifices and the amount of mental torture they went through during my times of trials. It didn't occur to me at the time to consider how much it might hurt them to say good-bye to me as I started a new life in an entirely different country far away from them. I know now how much pain it can cost you to watch your child suffer, to see her dreams crushed, to say good-bye to her. Now that I have a child of my own, I understand how my whole heart beats for her happiness. I see now how worried and desperate my parents must have felt while I was going through the prison time, the solitary confinement and torture when they couldn't even gain access to me or news of me, and the county prison when they could only visit me once a week for seven minutes at a time. Every time, they had to see me dirty, malnourished, crawling with vermin, and quickly losing hope to depression. Now that I'm a father myself, I fully appreciate the heartache of parenthood and how my parents must have also missed their son every second of every hour while I was in the military, present in the face of a terrible war and never knowing which minute, if any of them, would be my last. Now, I know.

But this was 32 years ago, and I was just a young kid, though I thought I was wise enough to know all I would need to know. My heart was full of broken dreams and my body was filled with torture scars to remind me for the rest of my life how much I hated being in the environment that had become Iran. Like so many others my age, I felt old and worn down well before my time. I desperately wished to get the hell out of there and try my chances in another country. I was smart and determined; I'd already started my own companies and had achieved success with two very different types of businesses under severe circumstances. Surely, I could find a country where I could pursue my dreams, whatever they may be, without worrying about everyday life's arbitrary things. Some government somewhere must certainly be receptive to ambitious young men like myself, who wanted to help build a better life for all of us. All I could think about was the future, specifically my future, and what I was leaving behind was of so much less importance.

My friend Mehrdad finished his military service obligations at the same time I did. He wasn't entirely sure what he wanted to do with his life yet, but he definitely wanted to try something different. Like me, he hadn't been too interested in joining the military in the first place and just wanted to go somewhere far enough away that he wouldn't be randomly pulled into war. Hearing my dreams of going away to university, he decided to join me. We decided to leave the country together and try to start new careers. Our plan was to go to Turkey and apply to attend the university in Ankara. My dream was still to become an engineer and I felt sure, if I worked hard enough at it, I would be able to get in. From what I understood, they would not hold my prison term against me when making their acceptance decision like the universities in Iran would.

It took us a few months to get our passports, so I spent that time enjoying my family and friends who would be staying behind. This was a much different leave-taking than that first time. Then, Mom had to throw a made-up celebration, so I could see everyone one last time without letting anyone else know what was really happening. It felt like a lie to not tell anyone why I seemed sad, and it felt like an exclusion to not let them in on my excitement. Plus, that earlier time, I didn't know when, or if, I would see any of those people ever again. For all I knew, I might be killed in my attempt to cross and, best case scenario, it could be years before I could get myself settled enough to bring my parents and siblings to a more open country. Who knew if I would ever be allowed to return to Iran to see additional family members or if they would ever get the chance to leave to visit me. Back then, I never thought there would be a scenario where I could leave Iran and still retain the right to come back for a visit.

This time, I didn't have to sneak my way out of town. I had time to close out any remaining business, hang out with the people I loved, and stock up on as many good memories as I could find before Mehrdad and I left.

Finally, the passports arrived, and everything was in place. This time, I was crossing legally! It felt great. I gathered a few belongings, Mom threw a real going-away party, I collected the last of my remaining money, and my dad helped me gain some more. This time I deposited the money in a bank and transferred it electronically to an account I would be able to access from Turkey. It was such an amazing opposing backdrop to my memory of the previous failed crossing attempt where I had so carefully stitched money in hidden pockets inside my clothing before that terrifying and unsuccessful endeavor. Within a week, Mehrdad and I were ready to leave.

The day of departure finally arrived, and we were all at the airport saying our goodbyes. No trekking through snow-filled wilderness and riding horses out of the mountains for me! Most of my friends and some of my close family members were there. Tears were running down faces and smiles were flying off them at the same time. The thought of leaving the dark past had been marinating in my mind and soul for such a long time. It was hard for me to distinguish between the main goal and the task at hand, the higher education and not the travel or the adventure. My daily torment that had lasted now for so many years was about to end, once I got through that sliding door. Once I passed through that door, I would fulfill the promise I made to myself during all those lonely, cold hours in a small solitary cell in Khoy. I had ended my life of living on the edge with no real identity. I had survived my life as a captive soldier in the Iran Navy. Now, I was finally about to embark into my brighter future. Becoming someone I'd dreamed of all my life. It would all happen in just a few steps.

I pressed my dad against my chest while I hugged him for the last time and kissed my mother's wet cheeks before I turned toward the long corridor leading toward the flight gate. It didn't take too long before we were in the air and I started to relax. It really happened. I was really in the air and on my way to Turkey. No guards had shown up to arrest me, no soldiers to strip me of everything I owned, not even the pressure of knowing I carried all my worldly goods on my person. I had a friend by my side and had crossed that final step, the border of my country, finally on the journey I'd planned for so long. Again, I realized I'd been beaten, but not broken. Again, I was standing on my own and achieving my goals.

Overwhelmed by the mix of thoughts and emotions, I pushed everything aside and took a few breaths to clear my mind and appreciate how much I already missed my family. I felt a warm tear on my cheek as I looked down on the very bright collection of lights of my hometown, Tehran, from up above as I left it behind. Maybe forever.

Chapter 6

Ankara

Turkish delight

It had been heart breaks and broken promises for years. Since I was 15 years old, most of my plans and dreams had been shattered by the government's direct or indirect influence. Now, finally, I was out of the dark place. Although I was a little behind my ideal schedule and had been through many years of desperate attempts, I finally found myself in a free land. Ankara, Turkey, my land of dreams.

The day I arrived in Ankara, I simply stood in the spring rain outside the airport for a while, marveling at the scenes around me. I was amazed seeing all the people on the streets as we rode in a shuttle from the airport to the city center. They were all wearing colorful outfits. Women were wearing regular clothes, even jeans and t-shirts, without covering themselves in dark-colored hijabs. Boys and girls, men and women, and children were casually walking around and going about their daily lives without any fear of being hassled or arrested for their inappropriate clothes or committing the evil sin of holding hands. None of these scenes were normal to my eyes. I couldn't fully appreciate that this was now the reality I was in. It is amazing when a normal scene of modern free life such as this presents itself as unbelievable enough to make you feel like you're standing in another world. It wasn't until that moment when I realized I had never been released from prison back in Khoy. Instead of living within the barred walls of the prison, I'd lived in a city-sized prison with invisible bars of fear and oppression along with everybody else while I was in Iran.

In the city center, Mehrdad and I checked into a cheap hotel. We couldn't wipe the smiles from our faces, and, as soon as we got settled, we decided to explore the city. 'Settled', for us, meant essentially dumping our bags on the beds, taking a quick glimpse around at our new space, grinning at each other, then heading back out the door. Those first few days were spent just exploring and enjoying our newly found freedom. By the end of the week, we started looking into apartments to rent. After all, the main goal was to go to college. I knew keeping the main goal the focus rather than the adventure at hand would be a challenge. To make sure I didn't slide into the journey, I had to stop being a tourist and start living like a student.

It took us only a few weeks to find and lease an apartment. Since we didn't have much more than a suitcase each, it was easy and quick for us to move in. Back then, a rental apartment meant a 2- or 3-bedroom apartment with nothing else in it. Even the floor had no carpet or covering. It was just a cement tile throughout the house. The kitchen was a small room with two cabinets and a sink. Windows did not have curtains and there was a single light bulb to brighten the entire apartment. The rent amount was only 150,000 Liras, though, which was about $150. Not bad and we didn't need much. Still, we were going to need more than what we had with us.

As a prospective student, I did not have a work permit and therefore was not officially allowed to work. Realistically, I had to come up with a strategy to stay afloat financially. I still had some money in the bank, but I needed to support myself for however long it took me to complete my studies plus I needed to pay my school tuition. I couldn't ask my parents for more money or anything really. I had put them through enough already. I also had no friends here to help me start a third new business. My only choice was to find a job that paid under the table, where the employer did not care about the work permit or any other inconvenient paperwork. With the help of my landlord, I found such a job in the currency exchange market in downtown Ankara. Like any job of this sort, this one didn't pay much, but it was a sweet after school and weekend job, and it covered at least some of my expenses.

It took us a few months to purchase the furniture we needed for the apartment. We bought some used furniture from other students and some from a used furniture store. A few people were kind enough to just let us have some furniture they no longer needed. One of the first things I bought was my own bed. Sleeping on the floor still brought back terrible memories. I also bought a little desk to study from and together, Mehrdad and I found some chairs and a table for the living room. We'd purchased a portable camping grill for the kitchen and some used silverware and dishes from the used goods store. Thinking back, my life as a free man started in Ankara under nothing more than bare minimum living conditions, but I was more content here than I'd ever been.

Aware I'd been out of the academic world for a while, and that things might be different in Turkey than at home, I signed up for a pre-college preparatory class. Going through the class was easier than I expected. I was planning to go to METU, which was an English-speaking college, so I had prepared, and all courses were covered in English. However, going through daily life in Ankara was not as easy as I'd hoped. Although my mother tongue is Turkish, it didn't occur to me ahead of time that my dialect from Iran was extremely different than the Turkish spoken in Turkey. Not only that, but not many people in Turkey spoke English at the time. I had to learn the language of the population fast.

I met my first Turkish girlfriend on a beautiful summer day shortly after I'd started my college preparatory class. It was going to take a few months for me to finish the course and I still had to overcome the problem of speaking with the locals. I was strolling through the park next to my apartment enjoying the freedom of movement I had along with the joy of simply being outside. I came around a corner and saw her walking toward me in a beam of light. She was a slender Anatolian Turkish girl, tall, with straight dark hair swishing across her back. I can still picture how her green eyes flashed at me when she laughed, and how the sound always drew my attention to her exaggerated lips. She was simply beautiful. I used some silly line about the weather or the park at large to get her to talk to me that first time, but she was willing to carry on a conversation. She spoke very softly with a calming and reassuring voice.

As we walked around the park that afternoon, I learned she was 24 years old and worked as a third-grade teacher at the local school. She lived with her mother, but her father, who had been a big investor and a successful businessman, had passed away a few years prior. Before his death, he'd ensured she would be given control of several restaurants and hotels distributed through Ankara and Izmir, a beautiful beach town by the Mediterranean. Although she had all those responsibilities, she still made time for our friendship to grow.

Even while I studied for the college entrance exams and getting myself settled in the city, this amazing woman patiently taught me the local language and overlooked my constant financial limitations. By the time I was ready to take the college entrance test, I was both ready for the test material and I was fluently speaking the Turkish language in Turkey. By mid-summer, I'd passed the exam and got accepted to my dream university. I was now officially a student of a beautiful and respected university. Yes! I was finally a college kid at the age of twenty-two!

Although I was working as much as I could at the money exchange office, it was still only part-time and low-paying, so I was poor, and money was always tight. I had about $3,500 to my name. With some desperation, I had invested those funds in a very risky bond that paid $150 a month as interest. My salary totaled less than $100 a month. I had to pay for rent, school tuition, books, food, clothing, and, occasionally, some fun at the local bar or pizza joint. Because even that was something of an extravagance, my entertainment usually consisted of nothing more than a six-pack of German beer and hanging out at home with my girlfriend, Gulay, and my roommate Mehrdad.

Months passed, and I became deeply engaged with my schoolwork, determined to place high in the class but never realizing my friendship with Gulay was slowly dimming. We saw each other less and less as the coursework increased in difficulty. By the following summer, we hardly saw each other at all. When she called and invited me to come out to dinner one night, I thought it was to officially break off our friendship. Her purpose certainly surprised me.

It was after dinner and the night was warm, so we decided to take a walk through the city. With an intimacy we hadn't enjoyed in a while, she slipped her arm through mine and leaned in close.

"Kamran, you know I love you," she said, those amazing lips tilted up to my ear.

I had no idea what to say. Searching my heart, I knew I liked her and I greatly appreciated all the help she had given me, but did I love her? Before I had much of a chance to say anything, she rushed on.

"I know you want to finish your studies, but if we got married, you wouldn't need to work so hard," she said. "You could live with me and stay here full-time. We could just live together and be happy. You wouldn't even have to work. I could sign ownership of some of my properties and gas stations to you."

She seemed ready to continue going, but I had to stop her. As tempting as she made it sound, I couldn't do that to her. When I got into a full-time relationship like that, I wanted it to be full of love, real, genuine, love like my parents had for each other.

"Gulay," I said, using a tone of voice I knew she would listen to. "You are a beautiful woman and I like you very much. I appreciate the help you have given me. I know I would not be doing as well as I am without your assistance. But I cannot marry you or take anything from you. I'm sorry, I do not love you as you love me."

There were tears and more talking. She even got angry, but that was the end of our friendship. We never saw each other again, but I always wished her happiness.

The summer months kept me busy with work in the currency exchange office in downtown Ankara. With the extra work, I had a little bit extra money so was able to get out and enjoy myself more with friends and schoolmates. After all those torturous days in Iran, I was finally tasting the real flavor of a normal life. I was living the dream of my youth as a single college student enjoying the bright spring days of his adulthood. It was not by any definition extravagant. But I didn't need extravagant. I needed to live in peace. To smile when I wanted to. To listen to my favorite music. To dance. To live. To just walk in the streets without worrying about being hassled or arrested for stupid reasons.

Things were going so well, I'd finally fully relaxed into the idea that I had achieved the perfect life and all my troubles were behind me. From then on, things were going to be an easy ride. Sure, I'd have a struggle here and there with exams or other minor things, but all the tough stuff was behind me.

As summer came to a close, though, I was once again proven wrong. A new chapter of my life started to take shape and, again, it was nothing I was planning for.

My friend and roommate Mehrdad who accompanied me from Iran to Ankara had not been as lucky as I had been. After two unsuccessful tries at the university entrance exam and struggling to make ends meet with a similar low-paying job to mine, he decided to pack up and go back to Iran and try his luck there. At least there he could get a real job and maybe save up enough money to make another try at it in a semester or two.

As Mehrdad grabbed his things to go back to Iran for an indefinite amount of time, he asked me to keep an eye on his girlfriend, Farzaneh, for him in his absence. He wanted me to make sure she got any help that she needed in his absence.

Throughout the previous summer, I'd had plenty of opportunities to get to know Farzaneh and her family. They were all waiting for their green cards to get processed so they could travel to the United States. Not only was Farzaneh my roommate's girlfriend, but they were also our Iranian neighbors. Her mom would cook for all of us each Sunday. We'd all gather in their apartment and shared afternoons filled with good food and awesome memories. Farzaneh was a beautiful, smart, funny, 20-year-old. She was also hot! But, she was my best friend's girl so strictly off-limits for all time.

I had to constantly remind myself she was Mehrdad's girl with Mehrdad there. When she and I stood together saying good-bye to Mehrdad at the Ankara train station and she huddled into me for warmth in the cold mist, I knew the challenge had just become real. I tried hard to stay away from Farzaneh, but Fate had a different plan. The day after we said goodbye to Mehrdad at the train station, we decided to take a walk home through the park. A sweet, long walk back home.

We hung out together every day after that for the next few months. We talked for hours, walked with no destination in mind, and shared laughs and smiles all day. We were friends, and I missed her beautiful brown eyes every time I said good-bye for the day. One chilly winter day in 1988, while walking aimlessly in a local market, she slid her hand through my arm, leaned over and softly pushed the side of her body against me. I felt the rushing of my blood through my body and my heart started beating fast. The world seemed as if it paused for a moment. She looked up into my eyes with her beautiful brown eyes and long curly lashes. She took my breath away. That moment was the moment I knew I had fallen for her. I knew with all my heart that I loved her desperately.

The next few weeks flew by and her departure date arrived before I could catch my breath. Her green card was finally approved, and she had to move to the US to be with her family. There was no stopping or delaying the process, and she had to leave. Fortunately, she was the last one to get her green card, so her family was already gone. That meant we could have a relatively private good-bye right there at the airport. Again, she looked up at me with those liquid brown eyes and curly eyelashes and I lost my heart. Our last kiss seemed branded into my chest in its place.

I hadn't even left the airport behind me when I knew I would not be able to spend my life without her. I somehow had to get myself to her in the US or wherever else she might go. Over the next few weeks, I researched the several different US visas available for foreign citizens. Most of them did not include Iranian Nationals. There was only one kind of visa available for Iranian students and it was called, appropriately enough, "The Student Visa".

I collected all the documents necessary for the visa and made an appointment with the US consulate in Ankara. I clearly remember the night before my appointment even though I was burning with a high fever and sitting next to my electric space heater, trying to get warm, watching the heavy snow showering the entire world around me. I stayed awake all night shivering with that fever and afraid to go to sleep in case I didn't wake on time for my morning appointment. The light of morning finally filled the sky. I put my best clothes on and dug my way through the snow to the bus station. Despite the fever and my worries, I found myself with a nervous smile in front of the embassy hours earlier than my appointment time.

Someone called my name over a speaker, the front gate opened, and I entered the structure. Again, I had uncomfortable flashbacks of the prison back in Khoy, but I pushed forward. Soon after, I found myself sitting in front of a thick glass with a black phone on either side. A middle-aged man sat on the other side of the glass window and did not look up as I sat across. He finally gave me eye contact, pointed to the phone and motioned for me to pick it up. As I picked up the phone, he asked for my documents. I pushed them through the little opening at the bottom of his window and the nerve-wracking interview started.

Hours later, I felt heavier than a truck as I pulled my sick body through the thick layer of snow in the alley leading back to my apartment.

"How could he deny my Visa?" I moaned to myself.

I kept going over it in my head.

"I had every little document ready, I was a great student. I had my records to prove it."

All my dreams seemed to be crushed, once more. My life was over without Farzaneh. It didn't matter what I might have accomplished in getting accepted to and successfully completing my first year of college, getting out of Iran, surviving the military, and living through the experience of the

Khoy prison structure. It had all been to get me to her, and now it seemed my path had been stolen from me again.

A few more days passed. I felt imprisoned in my body. It seemed to me I was meant for something I had not yet achieved. No matter how many of my goals were accomplished, there was always another impossible step I needed to take before I could find happiness. My next step was now to get to my love. Clearly, I was meant to move on once more. So, I devised another plan.

Chapter 7

Desperate measures

Walking into the shadow world

The US consulate, like my own government, refused to allow me to pursue my heart. First, my career was taken from me, now my love. They would not approve my simple student visa. I had no choice but to seek an alternative path to Farzaneh. For that I needed money. Lots of it. As a foreign student in Turkey, the only jobs I could get paid minimum wage at best. It was only enough to cover the most basic of living expenses. Even working two or three part-time jobs, I realized I would never make enough money to finance my next adventure, not before I hit old age anyway, assuming nothing ever went wrong. So, I approached the creditor who held my initial investment money and asked him for advice.

I was not too shocked to learn he led a team of professionals who accommodated fake travel documents for refugee families fleeing war-torn Iran due to political or social complications. His kindness and his fairness in working with me so far let me know he was at least sympathetic to our problems and truly wanted to help. I thought he might be able to refer me to someone. The real surprise was learning it was his team that was directly involved. His team's main goal was to relocate low-income refugee families into major European countries by providing them with fake passports, travel documents, air tickets, and start-up money. Even to this day, there is not a single official foundation or an international group helping Iranian families around the world to be relocated and reintroduced to a new society where they are safe.

I don't know who was actually financing the entire operation, but as far as I was concerned, their agenda was noble. By helping them, I could help expats, migrants and refugees to eventually have a future and a peaceful life as a family in a safe environment and at the same time, I could earn enough money to pursue my own plans while I was still young enough to reach them.

In less than a week, I witnessed creating fake documents using a mix of chemicals and ink products. They also had an electric typewriter, a tabletop foiling machine, and a laminating machine on hand to complete the passport and ID cards once the residues were washed off. I had one major responsibility within the company, escort the families to the airport and work as a translator.

Every morning, I walked into a smoke-filled, three-bedroom apartment three stories below street level in central Ankara. It was filthy and dark, having never seen natural light. The smoke did not bother me, though, since I was smoking a pack a day in those days. I'd sit and read a brief story about the lives and people in each family they were trying to relocate. These were stories they wrote themselves and forms they filled out that provided information such as weight, height, age, eye color, and other basics. Once I felt I had a feeling for who they were, I'd feel comfortable accompanying them to the airport or train station and help them along the way to not get caught for minor miscommunications. They tried to get families moving on as quickly as they could, so the family could start to recover from their experiences and begin creating new lives from a stable platform. This was especially important for the families with young children. The earlier the team could get them settled, the less impacted they hoped the family would be by the early crisis.

Although my official responsibility was to take the family to the airport and guide them through the various inspections and gates they needed to traverse, but mostly I just helped to keep the young ones busy and distracted from blurting out inappropriate answers while going through these formalities while keeping the parents' nerves settled. The most challenging age group to work with were the pre-school and kinder ages, with their innocent desire to be always honest yet their haunted eyes and fearful looks that gave away even more than their words. Sometimes I had to interfere more intensely. Either because the parents were not able to handle their nerves, something seemed off with the travel arrangements, or something seemed suspicious in the air, it was sometimes necessary to abort the plan for everyone's safety. It was also my job to know how to do that safely, in an inconspicuous way, so that no attention was called to our behavior.

I had the opportunity to meet many families during my short-lived work in the shadows. I heard stories about their sufferings and the way they were persecuted by Iran's government and the Islamic quasi police forces.

There is one couple I still think about, Farid and his very shy wife Shirin. I was surprised to see they had each been through the same prison system I had back in Khoy, caught trying to illegally cross the border. Farid and I had many similar stories of the tortures we endured in the prison, but the differences made me realize my sufferings could have been made worse.

Farid and Shirin were Baha'I, a vilified faith to Islam. I had heard Baha'Is in Iran were suffering all kinds of tortures, random executions, and seizure or destruction of everything they owned. What I didn't understand was why they didn't just pretend outwardly to blend. It also never occurred to me to think their punishments might be any worse than the punishments the rest of us were getting.

"We could not gain employment anywhere, we were not permitted to apply for university, and we did not quality for any standard government benefits," Farid told me. "Almost all of our civil rights were stripped from us after the Islamic Revolution. Baha'I could be arrested at random, beaten, and imprisoned for no other reason than our faith."

"Why did you not just tell them you were Muslim?" I asked. It seemed a much easier solution to just go through the motions, at least publicly.

"One of our most sacred rules is that we don't lie," Farid answered.

I was shocked. "Not even to save your very lives?"

"It is impossible," Shirin said quietly from the corner. Somehow, her voice carried more authority than Jahan's. While I might have kept arguing with him about it, her word fell like law between us.

My eyes dropped down to the hands she had neatly folded in her lap. She had several gray and dark purple marks all over what were seemingly once beautiful hands. As soon as she noticed me seeing them, she pulled her hands back, trying to cover them with her sleeves. I had a suspicion of how and why she had been burned. She truly was willing to die before uttering a lie. Understanding this, I suddenly understood why their situation had become so impossible.

The law would not allow them to work, get an education, or even receive government benefits. They were not permitted to leave the country and were prevented by their religion from lying to obtain fake passports. The only options left to them were to slowly starve to death waiting for Islamic forces to catch up with them and make them the latest brutal sport or to try to sneak across the border into Turkey and seek asylum in Canada.

As Farid and I shared stories about what had happened to us in Khoy, I came to realize that my beatings were not actually the worst the guards could do, despite what I thought at the time. It was actually possible to be dragged by something more painful and humiliating than one's nostrils.

"More than any tortures I had to endure, I think what pained me most was hearing the screams of my wife from across the hall as they tortured her," Farid said quietly with tears in his eyes. "And later, the sounds of her cries when she thought no one was paying attention. It was not just physical pain, it was mental anguish at what they had done."

"Is that what happened to your hands?" I asked Shirin, finally feeling bold enough with them to ask the question.

She took a deep breath and I didn't think she was going to answer. She looked away, into the distance between me and Farid as if she was searching through the dark memories and shadows of a tumultuous young life she'd rather forget. With luminous eyes, she looked down and began to speak.

"They are some of the cigarette burns the guards at the prison gave me when I refused to convert to Islam," she said. "Every day, they dragged me out to the yard, three, four, maybe more times. I still fear the daylight hours. Any moment I expect them to come beat me."

Although she was talking about a highly emotional topic, she spoke as if she was telling a story about someone else. None of the terror or pain was reflected in her face, which had become flat and expressionless, except for the tears that came rolling in fat drops down her cheeks. I could hear Farid pacing back and forth in the background. I couldn't imagine the pain he was going through as she described some of the tortures they'd inflicted on her.

"I can tell you how many times they beat me. Every time, I thought I would not last. I thought they would beat me into unconsciousness. But they never allowed me the relief. They would splash water on my head and slap my face. Then they would ask me, would I convert and they would burn another hole in my body. To know how much I was beaten, I just need to count the burn scars on my body."

The night they left for Canada, the entire rescue team celebrated and wished them a happy future.

The stories of the families I got to know firsthand were so familiar. If I hadn't suffered through it myself, friends, families, neighbors, had. It was all so close to home for me. I lived through the same events and I could feel their pain. I shared their sleepless nights filled with anxiety and nightmares. I could taste the bitter undertone of their hopeless voices when they reluctantly retold the stories of the torture they suffered. I carried my own scars with me all the time. I was indeed one of them. I belonged to those families and they were part of me.

When I started working in that dark and dingy apartment, my only incentive was to make quick money so I could be with my Farzaneh. Within a few weeks, it had turned into something so much more. Understanding that I was part of a much larger experience was strangely soothing, an emotional experience of connection that became part of me forever. In the eight weeks I worked for that little non-profit organization, I partially helped 14 families to finally abandon their tragic pasts in Iran, and find new lives in many major European countries. There, they were treated like human beings, provided initial food and shelter, and, eventually, with job opportunities and social immersion programs. All those kids who were only four- or five-years-old then are now in their mid-thirties. I hope they are now educated, healthy, and successful adults. My heart warms up as I think back to those days and what the outcome must have been for them. I wonder sometimes if they, too, remember me.

Meanwhile, I called Farzaneh as frequently as I could. She seemed very happy to rejoin with her family during our first phone calls. During the next two months, she started back to school and was doing well in her classes. I missed her a lot but knew I would soon find a way to get to her. I knew my turn was coming, and I had to make sure she shared the same feelings. So many times, my dreams had been pulled from me at the last minute. So many times, I could see the light of happiness just ahead, only to be blocked by the shadow of a guard's boot. This time, I had seen the passage to success; I had walked people through it over and over, without taking that final step onto the last plane. Now I wasn't worried as much about being caught as I was that my feelings were betraying me.

I knew it was possible I was simply building a dream life in my head based on a one-sided or possibly short-term love. I was risking so much to be with her. But what if she didn't really want my attention? What if she'd simply been trying to give me hope? What if her feelings had changed?

Within nine weeks of starting my job at the non-profit, it was my turn to relocate.

"You know I love you, right?" I asked her on our last phone call before my departure date.

"Of course," Farzaneh said, a little tease in her voice.

"Do you love me?"

"Of course," with that same teasing note.

"Do you love me enough to marry me?"

I couldn't believe those words had come out of my mouth. My heart stopped beating in my chest. I meant it from the depth of my being, but did I really just ask her to marry me over the phone?

That moment of silence seemed to last years. There was nothing in the world except the sounds of her breathing on the other end of the line.

"Of course." The teasing note was gone, but there was a tremor in it now, like she wasn't sure she knew what she was saying.

"Do you mean it?" I needed to know she'd considered it.

"Yes!" she yelled into the phone, her tone clearly excited and happy.

"We're going to get married," I said, feeling a sloppy grin spread over my face.

"We're going to get married," she affirmed.

I was over the clouds happy for the next several days. Finally, departure day arrived. I was due to fly out of Turkey that morning. My documents were ready, and my travel plan was decided. All the elements of the journey were in place. I grabbed the few things I owned and hugged all my friends at the non-profit good-bye. They were called angels so many times by those refugee families, and now they were my angels as well.

Destiny was calling, and I was ready to finally join my love. I couldn't wait to look directly into her beautiful brown eyes. I would tell her how I missed her, and I loved her with all my heart, forever. I would ask her again, in person, to marry me just so I could see the excited and happy look in her eyes, knowing already what she'd say.

All the steps were complete except the follow-through. It was a given that I would soon be settling into my dream life with my love at my side. Or so I thought

Chapter 8

The Lover Boy

Or

The International Criminal

When I was 13 years old, I spent most of my time thinking about the universe, death, and the meaning of life. Yes, I was a geek. I rode my motorcycle to the outskirts of the army base where we lived and watched the invisible summer wind create magical waves of gold through the fields of wheat. I could lie back in the middle of that field and drown in the majestic vastness of the blue sky. When it rained, I would write poems and walk under the clouds, brooding. I was quiet and very shy. I got embarrassed easily. The blood rushed into my head, turning my face a brilliant red, and my body started sweating at any simple unrest in my daily life. I was considerably overweight and was always bullied at school. They called me "The Barrel" thanks to my unfortunate shape. Nothing I did ever seemed to improve it.

My sister was my defender. Being a year older than me and a lot tougher, she felt it was her responsibility to defend her fat little brother, the Barrel, before the entire middle school. I hated forcing her to defend me all the time and being an embarrassment to her, so I did my best to keep a low profile. I was rarely interested in getting to know new people and tried to stay away from gatherings, even family parties. The more I crawled into the shadow my lonely world the worse I got.

In those days, I lived my life in fear of change and unfamiliar events. Nightmares and midnight shivers were part of my life, but I kept them all to myself. It was important to me that I not cause any more trouble for my family than I already was. I'm not sure why I always felt I needed to apologize simply for being me. All that started to change at the beginning of high school. I'd grown much taller and became a lot thinner. I was feeling a little more confident physically. All my demons stayed inside me, for I was a mouse in the lion skin. Yet, I allowed my new found physical powers to turn me into a mean boy who was determined to exact revenge on all those who bullied me during middle school.

I was prevented from becoming a brutal bully starting the day the revolutionary forces declared victory. That was when the army of angry and disgruntled solders rushed into our little community at the army base bent on destroying everything they could.

On that cold winter day, hearing the commotion coming from down the street, I was afraid for myself and my family. I was shocked beyond belief to witness such an astonishing and unfamiliar event. It was like witnessing an entire car crash with all its details, close up. I was frozen. When I could see them, they were running toward our house with torches in one hand and automatic rifles in the other. They were, at that moment, all those monsters in my head from childhood coming alive. I closed my eyes, ready to be crushed by the angry mob. It occurred to me in that moment that I could either die like an animal caught in headlights, simply standing there begging to be stuck, or I could fight for my life and the lives of my family.

I had no choice but to face the monsters. I was ready to face my fate. As they got closer and closer to me, the noise of their angry chants faded more and more in my ears. I closed my eyes and found total silence. I was in peace. I felt the heat of their torches in my face and inhaled the dust of their rampage. Yet, I didn't move. Something happened to me that day. Strangely, fear had turned into a peculiar form of peace.

When I remained untouched despite their closeness, I opened my eyes to watch them pass by me. I stood in the shadows, but, as they moved on toward my house, I had a sense they weren't really looking to physically harm people. They just wanted to frighten us. I witnessed some of them torch my motorcycle parked in the driveway. Some threw rocks at the windows of the house. A few of them grabbed my charred bike and threw it up in the air. Flames were everywhere around us as some of the buildings had been set on fire. The wave of angry mob was going from one house to another, destroying everything and anything they got their hands on, but not attacking the people running from the houses as long as no one in the mob was attacked. My family and my neighbors tried to keep a low profile as the mob marched through. Even as I watched the base burn, I smiled in victory. I was no longer afraid. I faced my fears and now everything was clear.

A few nights later, 15-year-old me was on the roof of my house with my father, both of us pointing Kalashnikov rifles toward the distant green hill across the field from my house. We were waiting for Kurdish separatists to attack the base. This time we seemed to be organized and prepared to mount a counter-offensive. My hands were trembling, and I was breathing fast. But I was not afraid. It was the adrenaline of my first anticipated battle pumping through my veins, and the knowledge that I was directly protecting my family, my mother, sister, and little brother tucked into a safe room we'd crafted inside the friend's house. At the time, I didn't know it was adrenaline and I was confused as to why my body was shaking the way it was when I was not feeling fear.

My father put his warm hand on my back. From his hand, his quiet peace warmed my whole body and soul. I felt strong and determined, as long as I had him next to me.

“Stay calm,” he said softly. “I’ll never let anyone hurt you or our family.”

He was a colonel in the army. There was no reason to think it might not be within his power to protect me. To the core of my being, I believed him. Our eyes met in understanding and faith.

"Let’s defend our family, let’s defend our house,” he said then. “I’m counting on you.”

My heartbeat returned to its regular rhythm. I realized my hands were not shaking anymore either, and I had a powerful grip on the rifle.

Those days, and especially that night in the heat of the battle, as terrifying as they were, forced me to come out of my scared little shell and grow into a stronger me, into someone I believed I was supposed to be for the rest of my life. The events of those dark days early in my life helped prepare me to survive the war, bombings, deaths, and public executions that followed. I built the tools I’d need to overcome prisons and torture. Those days of my early teens made me ready for many unfortunate and perilous events in the years to come.

Now, years later, I was about to start another chapter in my life as I prepared to cross another border. This time, I was to leave Turkey rather than Iran, but I was again about to cross the border illegally, using fake documents and a false name. Traveling to the US was supposed to be a smooth endeavor, but on the day of the first leg of the trip, my excitement turned into nervousness and doubt. I had done this so many times for refugee families over the past eight weeks. I'd been assured they'd all reached their final destinations without trouble. But now that it was my turn, my body and mind wouldn't settle down. All my senses were heightened. Every single memory of my past failed attempts to cross borders illegally rushed through my head on an almost endless loop. I could not get my inner thoughts to shift gears and feared I would become completely lost in the darkness of my own fears again.

I countered these endless loops by thinking about the life I'd had up to that moment. I thought about the events I'd survived, the terrible treatment I'd already overcome. All at once, what was in front of me did not seem that dangerous. The fear of crossing Turkey's border with a fake Spanish visa paled in comparison with what I'd been through already. I held my head up, looked forward, and smiled. I got this!

After a long 30-minute wait in line, it was finally my turn. I walked directly toward the officer with my passport in hand, trying to look confident and assured. Despite having walked refugee families through this process 14 times in the past eight weeks, helping them overcome their emotions as they went through this exact process, I realized how much more difficult it was to look normal when you are actually standing in their shoes. My facial muscles were not under my control. I tried so hard to hold a smile on my frozen face, but I couldn't tell what expression I might be wearing. I wished there was a mirror behind him so I could check myself.

The officer asked, "Where are you traveling?"

"To Madrid" I replied.

He looked at my passport photo and fanned through the pages. He paused over the visa page. He checked the visa stamp closely and looked up at me. I was trying so hard to keep the smile on my face, but it was getting more and more difficult all the time and felt more awkward the longer he stared. I tried to keep myself from breathing too fast. I'd trained myself to recognize the danger signs. I knew about how long this process should take, but there wasn't a clock on the wall. When time stands still, how do you know when you've crossed that 'too long' moment?

I was really trying hard to look normal. I felt my upper lip shuddering uncontrollably.

I think I've been trying to hold this smile too long, I thought. *Maybe I should stop smiling now. Maybe that would make me look more suspicious. What would be the best expression that isn't a smile? What would be normal?*

The silence was deadly and lasted way too long. I could feel sweat start to form on my back and neck. This process that I'd walked so many others through successfully was not going to work for me. Just like prison, when other guys got time for the same crime, they were released so much faster than me. He knew the visa was a fake, I was sure of it. They never took this long to approve someone.

He rubbed his finger on the stamp like he thought he could wipe it off. He stood quietly looking at it for some time. Finally, he looked up and smiled.

"Spanish girls are so hot, have fun," he said.

He stamped the passport with the exit visa and handed it back.

I was good to go! I could breathe again! With a spark of joy blooming in my heart, I made my way to the flight gate.

I landed in Madrid on a freezing cold afternoon. I walked right off the gate and toward the bathrooms as instructed. I was to look as if it was a moment of some urgency, so I didn't spend a lot of time looking around from the gate to the nearest restroom. I sat in the bathroom, held on to my carry on, and counted the minutes trying not to wonder more about where I was. The plan was to wait there for 30 minutes for the arriving crown to be disbursed, and then walk out and look for a coffee shop called "La Caprichosa". I wondered if it would take me long to find it. I hoped I wouldn't miss my connection and I reassured myself I'd already crossed the first and most difficult hurdle. The rest was just a matter of following the steps I'd already been given.

As it turned out, the coffee shop was easy to find since it was the only one in that terminal. I sat in the shop for a while wondering, hoping, I hadn't missed my contact. Did I get the timing wrong? I was so ready for something wrong to happen. It was almost as if I was looking for it. The barista brought me a second cup before my contact finally arrived. As planned, I recognized her by the purple jacket she was wearing. It was close to the same shade of purple shirt I was wearing.

She approached my table with confidence.

"Your passport?" she asked, holding out a hand as she slipped into the seat across from me. She sounded very official and businesslike. Her accent was eastern European.

I handed over the booklet. She brazenly went through the pages of my passport and found the next blank one. Right there in the coffee shop, where anyone could see, she applied a Cuban visa stamp.

"Your boarding pass," she asked again, handing back the passport.

Again, I simply supplied what she asked for.

This time, she didn't do anything to the pass itself other than tuck it into an envelope she was carrying, choosing another card from the interior.

"Take this," she said, handing it over. "You have a stop in the Dominican Republic before you arrive in Havana."

I thought she was done, but she sat there for a few moments, just looking at me. When I glanced down, I noticed she'd quietly pushed a piece of paper across the table toward me. The note provided the address and timing of my meeting with the next trafficker in Havana. I carefully added it to an interior hidden compartment in my wallet and she nodded her approval. She gently scanned around the coffee shop with her eyes before she got up and walked away. I was surprised by her confidence and accuracy.

All of this reminded me of the spy movies I'd watched as a kid, except I'd never imagined myself in the role of the hero. If nothing else, I knew I was no spy. This was not a life I wanted to be a permanent part of.

Checking the boarding pass and the flight boards, I learned I had a few hours to kill before my next flight departed. All my senses were telling me to lay low at the gate and just wait for the departure, but I couldn't resist walking around and browsing the duty-free shops. As I lost myself in the luxuries offered in the shops, I neglected to pay much attention to where I was actually wandering.

That proved to be reckless and stupid. I don't remember how I managed to go across a small gate in the duty-free shop that pushed me into the unsecured area. One second I was in the store, the next second I was staring at the outer terminal, outside of the transit area with no easy way back in. Of course, I immediately tried to go back through the gate, but it only turned in one direction, out. It was specifically designed to not allow me to go back through. I knew I had screwed up, I didn't think I could possibly get back through security again, not with the new boarding pass and all. I felt really stupid. I had to jump back into the transit area to continue the journey. It was all I could think about. I waited for a busy moment in the store and in the terminal and approached the gate. It was only a few feet tall. My plan was to throw my carry on over and then jump over myself before anyone noticed my actions. Before I could throw the carry on over, though, I felt someone's hand on my shoulder. In dread, I turned back, desperately hoping it was simply a regular passenger watching out for another. As soon as I saw the owner of the hand, though, I knew I was in big trouble. He was an airport security officer.

Within minutes I was hand-cuffed and moved into a holding room at the airport. All my plans had come to a crashing halt once again. My past experiences sent jitters through my body as I had no idea what to expect. Madrid was not a heartless Islamic regime, so I didn't think I would be tortured or beaten as I'd been in Iran, but I had no idea what to expect. Would I be going to jail for a long time? Would they send me back to Iran? After two hours of waiting in the room, watching the time of my flight come and go, an officer finally came in. With broken English, he told me they were going to transfer me to the downtown immigration holding cell.

I had my answer. I was going back to prison. My mind went back to a prison yard in Iran listening to one of my cell mate's advice. He was a soft-spoken thief and much older than me. In a voice roughened by years of smoking, he told me prison places a curse on all its residents.

"Once you manage to get yourself into one, you will come back," he said. "There is no escape. You will have that curse on you forever."

As I sat in the back of the police truck, all I could think of was the last time I was being transferred to a jail cell and what my soft-spoken cellmate told me on that cold winter day. My spirits fell into that mud puddle at the military compound back in Iran. My senses convinced me I was going back to Iran, back to the prison in Khoy, maybe never to be released again.

After arrival at the immigration holding cell, another officer interviewed me. I told him the stupid mistake I had made in accidentally crossing the gate in the duty-free store after getting turned around. I also told him I had no intentions of crossing into illegal borders at the airport. He was not convinced and rightfully so. I was holding a one-way ticket to Havana.

After the initial questioning, I was transferred to another area where the rooms turned into real jail cells, further convincing me I was ultimately headed back to Iran prisons. At least the cell looked clean, and there was a bed with no bedding and a table right next to it which was bolted to the floor. It was scant furniture, but it was better than the cold, cement floor. There was no window and the solid metal door had a small opening with bars going through it.

24 hours went by. I was able to go to the bathroom anytime I asked for it. They let me take a shower at night before curfew. Food was delivered on a tray and was decent. It was so different from the prison in Khoy except for one aspect. I kept asking what would happen next and did not get a straight answer. I was extremely frustrated, but I knew I should not make a fuss since nothing on my passport was legitimate. The best strategy was to be polite and play innocent.

Finally, on the morning of the second day, the door opened. The first officer to have arrested me came in. He told me to grab my stuff and that I was being released. Within an hour, we were back at the airport. The officer personally escorted me to the transit area and gave me a new boarding card to go to Havana.

"Let me give you an advice," the guard told me on the way to the airport, "you need to be much more careful in the future. Stay in the transit area at all times, unless you have a valid visa."

They knew all along I was breaking the law and yet they let me go anyway. Once I was back in the transit area, I sat on a chair at the gate and held on tight to my luggage. I wouldn't even risk going to a restroom just to be sure I stayed in a safe place. I took a deep breath and waited anxiously for the next chapter of my life. Again, I imagined I had finally crossed all the hurdles in my way. The rest of the trip had to be smooth. Nothing more could possibly go wrong. I had no clue that Havana would turn out to be an adventure like no other!

Chapter 9

Havana

A hell of a paradise

I changed planes during a short stop in the Dominican Republic, being very careful not to get sidetracked in any way. It was only a short flight to Havana from there. Even though it was a short flight, I was nervous something might go wrong on the other end. I crept to the back of the plane, just behind the bathroom, to smoke a cigarette. There was a small window back there I was able to peek through. Suddenly, the white and golden clouds we'd been flying above cleared away to reveal the lush green landscape of the island filling the entire view.

Shortly after that incredible view revealed itself to me, we touched down in Havana. It was the end of February 1988; the weather could not have been more beautiful. One breath and you were transformed by the smell of wet ground and the freshness of the cool breeze. Stepping down the stairs onto the Havana airport tarmac, I felt I was finally getting close to my love. As I stood there, I knew I was only 85 miles away from the US mainland. As worried as I was on the plane, the clear air here again filled me with hope for a better future.

Havana, as easy as this part of my journey was supposed to be, proved to be torturous and filled with its own number of misadventures.

My Cuban visa was legitimate. Iranian passport holders were permitted Cuban tourist visas for a short time. My visa was for two weeks, but I only needed two days. I was supposed to meet up with my trafficker the day after my arrival. He would give me a fake Mexican visa stamp and I would fly to Mexico that same night. It should have been so simple and straight forward.

However, since I was missing in action for three days in Spain thanks to my mistake in Madrid, I missed the original appointment. It didn't worry me too much, though, because we had made contingency plans. I was to leave a message for my contact person as soon as I arrived at the reception lobby of the Grand Hotel in Havana. My contact was supposed to check his messages on daily basis. If I didn't show up three days ago, he would not have been looking for me. Leaving my message today would just pick us up where we'd left off. This early planning kept me from being too anxious.

Our meeting place was the old and extremely classic Grand Hotel Saratoga Havana. A short 30-minute shuttle ride got me to the hotel. At a glance, it seemed perfectly preserved from the 40's. But as I got closer and finally got into the lobby, I could see the wear and tear everywhere. I didn't notice it at first, but I later learned Cuban citizens were not allowed to enter hotels hosting foreign visitors. There were also a few western style stores created for tourists only, so none of the locals were to enter those stores either. Just because they were not permitted to enter did not stop them from peeking through the glass doors and windows with a mix of curiosity and envy.

My hotel room was huge and extremely clean. The tall ceilings were covered with plaster veneer artworks. I didn't need a room this fancy, but my meeting place was in the lobby of the same hotel the very next morning. After all I'd been through so far, I didn't want to be late, lost, or allow anything else to prevent me from getting to that meeting. No phone numbers were exchanged between me and my contact. Back then, there were no cell phones available either. I did not speak Spanish and did not want to risk anything by staying anywhere else. So, as much as it was hard for me to spend such a high amount of money, I decided to pay the $75 per night required for two nights of stay. That was almost one month's worth of rent for my apartment back in Ankara.

I spent the entire night in this luxurious room nervously pacing back and forth. Would everything go as we'd planned? So far, nothing had been smooth. I hoped I would finally arrive in the US in less than four days. I was so tired of the travel, the uncertainty, the fear I'd been experiencing since this journey began. I hoped it would all be worth it in the end. I would finally meet up with Farzaneh and we would have a chance to live the happily ever after kind of life I'd fantasized about as a child. Given the cost of this hotel, I wondered what I was going to do when I did arrive in the United States.

Would I be able to work and go to school? How would I support our living expenses? I could not expect Farzaneh to live with me with all those uncertainties. Why didn't I think about these things before?

In the end, I realized that the sheer need of being with her had filled my entire body and soul. Any hardship would be worth even a short amount of time with her. So, I stopped worrying about the minor details and started fantasizing about the beautiful spring day in California when I would finally see her again. I could hold her in my arms and tell her how much I missed her. Tell her about my journey and how much it was all worth it just to see her smile again.

The meeting time with the trafficker was set for 9 am in the lobby the next morning. I was there an hour early. His name was Jahangir and he showed up with a big smile right at 9 am. I'm sure he recognized me by the worried look on my face. He never hesitated to ask me whether I was the person he was set to meet. He told me we had to wait for a few more people before he explained the plan.

Before too long, those few people showed up. There were a young couple and three more guys. After the introductions were over, Jahangir explained the plan. It was very elaborate and sounded extremely risky, but we were all here to do anything physically possible to get to the US. For most of us, anything was better than going back to where we'd come from.

Based on my past experience, great-sounding plans with poor execution resulted in very bad endings. This time, even the plan did not sound that great. However, we were all too far into this. Each one of us had incentive to overlook the flaws. We were almost there, and we could all see the light at the end of the tunnel. We all had our reasons. Mine was love, an awesome love.

Jahangir asked for our passports and told us he would be back the next day at the same time and same place with the fake Mexican visas attached and signed to each one. We were to check out and leave immediately after his arrival. Everything seemed to be going perfectly well. It was only another 24 hours before we would be on our way to Mexico and one step closer to our destinations.

I was tempted to get out of the hotel and walk around town. After all, when would I have another chance to visit Havana?

This is the perfect opportunity, I said to myself

But after what happened in Madrid, I decided to stick around the hotel compound and wait out the next 24 hours. No sense on taking unnecessary chances.

The next morning, I woke up very early and headed out to our meeting place a few hours early. I checked out and sat by the entrance door, waiting for everybody else. The other people in our group showed up early as well and, by the look on everybody's faces, I could tell they were as nervous as I was. Jahangir showed up right on time, causing us all to start up with anticipation.

When he walked in the door, though, he had an ominous look on his face. My heart skipped a beat. I'd seen that kind of look before. I knew for sure there was something wrong.

He approached us quickly and turned to one of the guys.

“Unfortunately, my Mexican contact did not bring enough visa stamps, so we could not get everybody’s passports ready,” he told him.

I couldn’t breathe. Every step along this journey had been full of disaster. I don’t know why I’d been feeling so hopeful.

As the other young man took in this news, Jahangir looked at me and gave me the bad news as well. They’d obviously decided to focus on getting the family out first. I wasn’t sure what should be my reaction. Jahangir was already paid for the job. This wasn’t exactly a regular contract where I could hold him accountable to finish. He had the money, he had the fake visas, and he knew all the contacts. I, on the other hand, had a Cuban visa that would expire in less than two weeks, no contacts, and a very limited amount of money and no means of getting more. I struggled to think of what to say, what the next question should be. But before I asked anything, Jahangir began speaking again, this time to the whole group.

"We did the passports for our young family first, before we ran out of visas. I will fly with them to Mexico this afternoon and return for the rest of you in a few days. For those of you staying behind, please be patient with me and do not talk with anyone if you can avoid it. Do not go out venturing the town."

He stopped for a moment to look each of the three of us staying behind directly in the eye before continuing. Apparently, this was very important.

"Just sit tight and I will be back for you, right here, in two days."

He seemed honest, but it didn't matter. I had no other choice but to trust him.

The young couple and their brother were very happy to leave, but they were trying hard to show empathy. At the same time, it was hard for the rest of us to show happiness for them. We were the ones being left behind. They grabbed their bags, waved goodbye and disappeared in the crowd outside of the hotel entrance with Jahangir.

Watching them go, I felt like a child whose father dropped him at the orphanage and promised to come back soon. Devastated but still hopeful, I went back to the lobby with my luggage to think. I knew I could not afford this hotel's room anymore. I only had a small amount of cash that was supposed to last me throughout the journey and get me re-established in the United States. The trip was already longer than I'd expected, and more expensive. Who knew how long my finances would need to last?

I knew Jahangir would not be back for at least another two days, if ever. Even though he'd warned us not to wander away from the hotel, I decided to venture out and find a more affordable place to stay. I needed to make my money last. I walked around town and tried to locate a place close to the Grand Hotel so I could be in its lobby as early as possible each morning waiting for Jahangir's return.

I finally found a hostel near the hotel. I had to share the room with a few other people on the second floor and we had a common bathroom. The place was filthy, but it was cheap. Twenty American dollars covered one-week of stay and daily breakfast. It seemed like a great deal. I had not eaten anything that day so far. I was very worried about the amount of time I had to spend in Havana. I needed to save any little amount of money I could and decided to wait until that free breakfast to eat rather than spending my dwindling funds on a dinner.

The next morning, I pounced on the breakfast table after 24 hours of mandatory fasting. I still remember that breakfast table. It was a long and narrow metal table covered with a simple white cloth. Toast, butter, boiled eggs, and bananas were placed along its length. I filled up on eggs and bananas before going for a long walk around town.

The weather became hot and unbearably humid in a matter of a couple of hours. The beautiful promise of the morning had turned sour, just like my simple and straight-forward plan to go to Mexico.

Most of the buildings in Havana were still standing from the 1940's and 50's, most with the help of large wooden boards and anchors keeping them from crumbling. Paint was peeling from all of the buildings, telling stories of years of rain and heat and humid weather with no maintenance. At first glance, most of the downtown buildings looked like old hotels and casinos, still hosting the ghosts of rich American patrons drinking fancy spirits and laughing at their winnings and fortunes, but as I got closer and peeked inside, I realized big rooms and lobbies had been sectioned off by curtains, dividing them into single quarters where entire families lived. They shared the bathroom and shower and cooked at the old public mess hall of the building.

The streets were quiet, and I could see long lines of people in random queues in front of different buildings. As I got closer to each line, I could see that they were in line to get different things like food or supplies. It reminded me a little of the lines I used to stand in to get things for my family back in Iran. But I couldn't see where there was any exchange of money or vouchers of any kind. The items were more like handouts. I sat for a while and watched the progression of a line that was apparently for citizens to get shoes. Each person would receive a pair of matching shoes once they arrived at the window in the front and then they'd move away. They would then trade with others for the appropriate size on the side of the street nearby, making it clear that they had no choices when it came to getting what they needed.

In another line, they were getting bags of bread and some were getting bags of sugar. There were smaller lines in front of smaller shops, but I didn't hang around long enough to see what they were getting. Later that day, I figured out that some of these shops were cigar shops and each Habanero and Habanera was allowed to get one cigar per day except on Sundays.

By early afternoon, I found my way to a huge waterfront roadway. I later found out it was one of the most popular hangouts for younger generations of Cubans and tourists. It was called Avenida de Maceo. Cubans and tourists alike flocked to this wide boulevard to watch the sunset. For some, it seemed a place to fantasize about crossing over the narrow patch of water to get to the United State. They stood staring longingly toward the not-so-far-away coast. I could certainly understand that as I was doing a bit of that myself. For others, it was a just a place to watch the sunset and wipe the tears of a broken heart. Or maybe all these feelings and observations were just me. I was in a sad state of mind. I sat on the cement retaining wall facing the Caribbean Sea and went into deep thoughts.

Hunger brought me back to the real world. It was already dark when I noticed the lines were forming again. This time, it was in front of a make-shift food counter. They were handing out a slice of something that resembled pizza, a paper bowl of ice cream and a plastic cup with an orange bubbly drink. I hesitantly jointed the line. I wasn't sure if they asked for an ID of some sort, but I hadn't seen any exchanges that would suggest it so far in any of the lines. People just stepped to the front and got what was offered. I hadn't had any food or drink since breakfast and anything I could get was welcomed.

When It was my turn, the lady behind the counter didn't even look at me as she handed me the triangle food. It was a piece of flat bread with tomato sauce smeared on top of it, no cheese. The cup of ice cream had blackened ripe banana pieces in it, and the orange bubbly was extremely sweet. It was a perfect!

After dinner, I followed a group of young Havanans to a park. I could see them pulling small bottles out of their pockets and sipping while walking. Soon, we arrived at the center of the park where a local band was playing reggae music. I sat with everybody else and tried not to think about my recent misfortune.

Two days passed that way and by then I knew I did not have to pay for food as long as I was in Havana. Hell, I could even get shoes, clothes and a cigar a day!

On the third day, I went to the Grand Hotel lobby right after breakfast and saw the other two guys from my group waiting as well. I usually did not smoke until the late afternoon, but the wait and anxiety forced me to smoke non-stop. I think I finished my first pack before the day was over. The entire day went by slowly as we all waited it out in the lobby, but there was no sign of Jahangir. I tried to speak to the other two guys, but they did not seem to be interested in talking to me. They, too, were frightened and worried and did not want to heighten their anxiety by sharing their stories with a stranger.

After midnight, I went back to my hostel only to repeat the same thing the next morning. Breakfast and right to the Grand Hotel's lobby. A few days passed like that and there was still no sign of Jahangir. At least I had two other people going through the same thing to reassure me I hadn't missed him. After a week, the guys approached me at the hotel.

"We cannot wait any longer," one of them told me.

"We have decided to go back to Turkey and try again," the other one said.

"We've talked about it and we do not believe Jahangir will return. He has already received all of the money and there is nothing we can do to get it back," the first one explained.

"You should come with us."

This was a great blow. I had completely lost my sense of optimism for Jahangir's return, but I didn't know what to do about it. I could not go back to Turkey. I had to get to Farzaneh and start our life together before she lost patience with me. I told them no and watched as they, too, took their bags, waved goodbye and disappeared into the crowd just like the others. This was becoming old, fast. Their departure significantly increased my sense of anxiety and, of course, my cigarette consumption. Although we did not share any conversation throughout the period of waiting and anticipating, having those other guys around gave me some sort of hope. After all, it was easier to leave one person behind forever than three.

By the third week, I was sure that Jahangir would never come back. I had to make a decision fast. My visa had expired, and I was now a target for any Cuban police. Money was running out, so was my patience. One of those nights when I went to the hostel, I was approached by two police officers. They asked me for my passport. I knew I was in trouble again. I was sure that the front desk clerk ratted me out. He had a copy of my passport with the visa expiration date. I pulled the passport out of my secure passport pouch and gave it to them. Minutes later, once more, I was handcuffed in the back a police truck.

A small, wet cell was waiting for me in this dark, smelly jail. I was kind of relieved that the police had already decided my fate and they would soon deport me to Turkey. At least I didn't have to blame myself for deciding to go back. I was sure that within a few short days, they would process me and send me back to Ankara. After all, I was not a criminal and was just a tourist with an expired visa.

Six days passed, and I was still in the Havana jail. The cell was smelly and wet as the rain was coming through an opening on the sidewall. There was no window and just a few bars. I couldn't believe I had gotten myself into yet another jail. This was becoming a routine for almost all the port of calls of my journey and I did not like it. At least I was alone in the cell this time and did not have to worry about other criminals sharing the space with me.

The seventh morning, I woke up in pain with a burning hot temperature. That was all I needed. I was sick as a dog. Coughing and sneezing, I called on the guards and asked for any help I could get. I tried so hard to make them understand that I was very sick, but they just listened and left with no reaction.

One more day passed, and my situation got worse. The ninth day, the guards finally realized that I was not well at all, and they did not want to deal with a dead tourist. I was transferred to a local hospital. I barely remember getting there and the X-ray room they took me to. Apparently, I passed out during the examinations and later was moved to a room in the hospital.

The next morning, I woke up feeling much better. My temperature was lowered but the coughing was still there. Two young doctors visited me and, surprisingly, they could speak English. They told me I had a severe case of flu and before it turned to something much more serious, I'd better stayed at the hospital for at least a week.

At this point, I was quite sure Jahangir was never going to come back for me, but I was still anxious about not being around the hotel lobby in case he ever did. So, I insisted on being released. The doctors told me once they released me, I would be placed back into police custody and either I would be deported immediately or sitting in a jail cell for few more days before getting deported.

Given my options, I decided to stay in the hospital as long as I could in the hopes that Jahangir would come back for me eventually and find me there. Little more than a week later, my free room and board at the hospital was over and once again I found myself in the police truck. This time, they took me to the hostel and told me I had 48 hours to get my stuff and fly back to Turkey.

I ran to the Grand Hotel lobby once I got out of the police car. The reception there had not heard about Jahangir or anyone else looking for me. Although I had prepared myself for the disappointment, I was still hoping for something positive. Distraught and tired, I went back to the hostel. I was facing another important decision. Should I give up and go back to Turkey, or should I try to find somewhere else to stay and wait longer for Jahangir? I picked the latter.

I collected my luggage and checked out. Again, I walked around town looking for an inexpensive place to stay. Originally, my stay in Havana was supposed to last a couple of days, but by this time, I had spent more than six weeks in Havana. My money, my hope, and my patience were about to run out. I was exhausted and all the while, no one knew what had happened to me. I had not been able to contact any of my friends, my parents, or even Farzaneh. Constantly hoping to get things back on track, I had not called home or Farzaneh since Jahangir told me I would soon have the visa to go to Mexico. I was sure they were worried sick, but I couldn't tell them all my plans were ruined, and I was stuck illegally in Cuba.

Aimlessly walking around town in my search for another hostel, I passed by an old hotel with giant glass walls facing the street. I noticed a bunch of young boys and girls sitting around the main lobby. They looked very Middle Eastern. Cautiously, I entered the lobby pulling my luggage with me. There was a bald older man reading through a list in his hand standing in the middle of everybody else. He was speaking Farsi and roll calling everyone's name. Each time he called someone's name, he asked him or her to pack up for the Mexico flight that afternoon. My heart was beating so fast. Could this be my way out? Was I supposed to be on his list? Did I miss him earlier at the Grand Hotel lobby?

Questions and the anxiety of the past several weeks of waiting and losing hope overtook my entire body. I could barely move or speak. Suddenly, the older man turned around, as if he felt the cold presence of me standing behind him. He approached me with a surprised look on his face.

"Can I help you?" he asked.

I couldn't make eye contact at first, but, in a momentary rush of courage, I decided to take control of my own story.

"Yes, you forgot to call my name."

The man's name was Samad and, after a brief conversation, I found out this guy had his own route of human trafficking. He had nothing to do with Jahangir. However, he knew that Jahangir had recently returned from the US and was in Mexico City waiting for a group of people to move across the border to the US. He told me I could catch up with Jahangir if I left that afternoon with the rest of the group.

There was, however, a huge problem. He could not take me to Mexico for free. I tried hard to convince him to take me with the rest of the group, and I would make Jahangir pay him as soon as we arrived in Mexico City. But he was adamant to get paid before helping me. He was asking for $1500. I had the last portion of my money tucked in my shoes, which only amounted to $1000. I also had a gold army ring that my dad gave me before I left Tehran. I offered him both and he accepted.

I finally got my passport the same afternoon with that illusive Mexico visa stamp and was on my way to the Havana airport along with 25 more passengers. At last, I was about to embark on my next adventure.

Chapter 10

"Mexico", A tale of two cities

On our way to the Havana airport in the shuttle bus, no one was talking. It was as if everyone was holding their breath until passing through Cuban immigration at the airport was safely over. We all knew we had fake visas. We also knew how big of a deal it was to get in that kind of trouble in the communist Cuba with their inexorable justice system. I'd had a very minor taste of it myself and didn't want to return to it. We weren't even looking out the windows, just staring straight ahead or at the floor, each of us captive inside our own minds.

We arrived a few hours before the scheduled flight and Samad gave us instructions before we left the van.

"Do not clump up as a group," he said. "It would be better if you were to scatter around the airport lobby in smaller pairs, no more than three people in a group. Also, try not to interact with any of the other groups. Act natural but stay cautious. We'll be on our way to Mexico before you know it."

But Mother Nature had different plans for us. Within minutes of unloading from the shuttle van, a tropical storm moved over the entire island and rain poured down like a solid sheet of water from the dark skies. All flights were cancelled until further notice, and we were forced to wait out the storm in the airport terminal.

Eleven hours later, I found myself literally chewing my entire fingernail off in nervous agitation. I hadn't even realized I was doing it. Others were not better off. The degree of anxiety and sheer panic was growing exponentially every hour that we waited for the unknown future. Police guards were walking around the airport lobby in pairs. Keeping normal facial expressions, as they had random eye contact, proved to be very difficult as the time passed by ever so slowly.

Finally, the weather cleared, and the flights resumed. We all got in different lines as instructed and kept our best touristy face as we approached the immigrations booth. We were told if even one of us got into trouble, that would alarm the immigration officials and all of us would be in trouble. With just one alert, all Mexican visas would be canceled for that flight.

While going forward in the long line, I purposefully tried to be the last person of the entire group to go through the immigration booth. My luck had been so bad so far, I didn't want to get caught simply because someone else hadn't made it through. I also didn't want to risk everyone else's dreams on the chance that my personal bad luck would continue to hold. Meanwhile, I kept looking over at the other lines using my peripheral vision. I planned to bail out if I saw a commotion of any sort. I wasn't going to get arrested again. No matter what.

It was finally my turn. I was the last person of the group. Everyone else had already gone through. I put a smile on my face and walked firmly toward the booth. I handed over my passport. The policeman opened it to the first blank page. Without wasting a second, he slammed an exit stamp on the page. He did not even look at my face. He shoved the passport back through the opening and looked at his watch. I said thanks and passed through. It was that easy. All that panic felt wasted.

Less than an hour later we were all boarded in the plane heading to Merida, Mexico. It seemed to me that we were still all holding our breath until the plane finally took off. I could almost hear the sigh of relief filling the entire plane as we left the runway. Once the seat belt sign turned off, one person of our group started clapping. We all looked at each other and all of us started clapping and laughing uncontrollably. I can't imagine what the other passengers must have thought. I was genuinely happy for the first time in months. I was out of Cuba and on my way to Mexico. One step closer.

We were told we would first land in Merida, but the plane would go forward from there to our actual destination in Mexico City. We weren't sure of the reason for this, but I thought perhaps it had something to do with smaller town, less stringent security.

"If you had a valid visa," our trafficker told us, "you would get off the plane in Merida with all the other passengers, walk to the immigration booths, get your passports stamped, and get back on the same plane to Mexico City."

I wondered if we were supposed to hide on the plane somehow to avoid this. Obviously, our visas weren't valid, and we could not go that route.

"Since you can't do that with your fake visas," the man continued as if he'd read my mind, "I want you to get off the plane in Merida just like all the other passengers. Follow the signs to the immigration booth like everyone else, just as if you were planning to go there. As you walk through the long hall to the booths, you will see a public bathroom about halfway along the length. Whether you need to use the facilities or not, go in there and wait."

"Just wait?" one of the guys asked.

I was thinking the same thing. It would be very strange to walk into a public restroom and find a bunch of guys in there just hanging out.

"No, pretend to be busy," the man said. "Use the stalls, wash your hands and face, make it look authentic, but stay in there until the rest of the passengers, the ones with the real visas, start to walk back. They'll have been through immigration and received their entrance visas. Once you start hearing them in the hall, you can start to filter out and head back to the plane.

"This is where it can be tricky. Women and men will not know when the others are coming out and we have to make it look natural. Try to come out one at a time. If you were in groups at the Havana airport, it is fine to be in those same small groups now, but do not switch traveling companions. Don't give anyone a reason to remember you."

So, basically, his plan for us was to simply skip the immigration procedure. It sounded really stupid. Wouldn't they check to ensure we'd received our visas before allowing us on the plane? Then again, I didn't know just how they did things here in Mexico. Maybe it was different than Turkey and Cuba. Maybe it could work.

We landed at the Merida airport a little after midnight following a very short flight from Cuba. All 250 passengers were required to disembark from the plane and go to the immigration booths for their entry stamps. My brief hour of happiness and relaxation on the plane turned instantly back into the stressful and familiar series of panic-filled moments just waiting to be caught.

Mixed in the crowd, we all walked slowly through a dimly lit, narrow, long, and curvy hallway just as we'd been told. I anxiously watched for bathroom signs and soon found one. The bathroom was, not surprisingly, busy with almost 20 people just from our group in there, plus other passengers from the plane. Everyone was nervously washing their hands or waiting in the stalls. Soon, the other men from the flight drifted away and there was no sound coming from the outside. We knew we had to wait for the crowd of other passengers to come back, but at least now we didn't need to pretend to be busy anymore. It was hard to stay still, and I waited for any minute when the Mexican police would come to sweep the restrooms.

Less than 15 minutes later, I heard people walking back toward the plane. A few of the guys from our group obviously couldn't wait to get out and mix with the crowd getting back on the plane. I was again one of the few people who waited to get out of the bathroom last. Once I got out, I noticed there was a line in front of the door at the end of the hall leading back onto the plane.

What is the line for? This was not part of the plan, I thought to myself.

There were a few police officers checking every passenger's passport for the required entry stamp. I was terrified. So was everyone else in the group. But we had no other option. The line was moving forward, and we were approaching the policemen, getting closer and closer to certain prison time. As we got closer, though, I noticed Samad standing right next to one of the policemen. The first person of our group approached the police. She was visibly shaking.

Samad whispered something into the policeman's ear. The woman in front of him paused for a second, and the police officer waved her through. I knew then that some of the money we were charged was for safe passage here in this little town in Mexico.

We all passed through as Samad pointed each of us out to the policeman. Once again, we were all boarded on the plane, this time toward Mexico City. This time as a domestic flight. At the other end, there was no passport control anymore. Once again, sheer happiness settled in and relief took over the entire group.

We arrived in Mexico City in the very early morning. A storm had passed, and the sun was peeking through the rain clouds as I left the plane and took a fresh breath of air on the tarmac. Although this was considered a domestic flight, I was still cautious, and I could see the same emotion on everybody else's face in our group. We were all entering the country illegally after all.

A short bus ride took us through the busy streets of Mexico City to our hotel. As I hauled my small luggage up the stairs of the hotel, I noticed the familiar face of Jahangir sitting in the lobby. I wasn't sure how to react. On the one hand, I was extremely happy to have successfully gone through another hurdle of my adventure and on the other hand, I was very angry and disappointed with him to have forsaken me for weeks in Havana.

He ran toward me as soon as he saw me and took my luggage, offering me help and lots of apologies. As a token of his apology, he got me a suite and promised me that he would never lose sight of me until we got to the US. He then got my money and ring back from the other guy and had a nice tray of food and a bottle of wine delivered to my room. I was being treated like a king after all I went through and it felt great.

Later that night, he explained that some miscommunication created the entire mishap of us being left in Havana for that long. The entire time we were waiting, while I was in jail and in the hospital, he was under the impression that the three of us left behind in Havana had already flown to Mexico and crossed over to the US with his partner's aid. What he didn't know was that his partner had moved another group of people entirely who had successfully crossed over to United States.

"We will stay here in Mexico City for at least a week before we can continue your journey to the US," he said.

"Why the delay?" I asked, starting to feel frustrated again. The longer I stayed here, the greater chance I had of getting into more trouble.

"We have to wait for an opportune moment. Which reminds me … " he looked at me sideways. "I need to ask you not to contact anyone over the phone while you are here."

"Why is that?"

"There are listeners everywhere. You could compromise our location and intent. They would catch us all."

For the entire week, we remained divided into groups of no more than three people. We were never in our entirety at one time in the same location. Each subgroup had a Mexican handler, and they were well coordinated. We were taken to different places for food and just walked around town like real tourists. We never stayed close to the hotel perimeter until late at night as we were heading to bed. We passed through the lobby to go to our rooms to sleep and, in the morning, did the opposite to go out and so forth.

The week passed very quickly. It was refreshingly calming and reassuring to have Jahangir and the other guys around at all times. I again started to relax. I even saw some smiles on the faces of some of the people from our group. We all knew the destination was in sight and sooner rather than later we would arrive at the final leg of our common journey.

The day finally came, and we all packed up one more time to take the shuttle to the airport. This time, the destination was Juarez on the border of Mexico and the United States in Texas. Boarding the plane went without an incident. It was a domestic flight after all. A few short hours later, the captain was diving for the landing strip at the Juarez airport, and we were all counting the hours to cross the border into United States of America.

Juarez, the sister city of El Paso, seemed calm and quiet. It was hot and dusty. American-made cars were cruising on the streets and it kind of made me feel that I was indeed at the end of my trip. We were shuttled to a travel lodge and were roomed in groups of three again.

We were asked to give over all our documents, including passports and any sort of identification. We were also asked to give them our entire luggage and even jewelry and watches. We were supposed to cross the border as light as possible. Literally.

It was early afternoon by the time they were done collecting our documents and luggage. Afterwards, we were asked to keep the door shut and wait for our handlers. It was a small and smelly room. All of us were quiet and anxiously waiting for the handler to show up. Curtains were drawn and windows were closed. It must have been very hot since all of us were sweeting bullets.

Finally, our handler opened the door and asked us to follow him. We followed him down the stairs and through the lobby. I could feel the penetrating look on most of the men standing in the hallway all though the hotel lobby, as if they all knew what we were up to. There was a taxicab waiting outside. We got in and, in a few minutes, we were parked right next to a very long concrete embankment of some sort.

"Get out," the handler said to us. "You are to climb the embankment and find your next handler waiting on the other side."

"You aren't going with us?" I asked. I was starting to feel very uncomfortable again, like something wasn't going quite right. But what could I do? They had everything.

Just like a bunch of scared little puppies, we got out of the cab, looked around and cautiously started climbing up the concrete embankment. Once at the top, I realized that we were on top of the wall of a canal that enclosed the Rio Grande River from both sides of the border. There was a Mexican guy in a semi-truck-sized inner tube waiting for us down the embankment on the river. He was holding on to a tight rope that was stretched across the river. He waived his hand and yelled, ”Andale cabron”.

It all seemed so unprofessional and sketchy, but we had no other choice. The embankment was slippery, and the dark colored and cloudy Rio Grande was roaring in the foreground. We made our way down to the inner tube and sat around it. The Mexican guy started pulling on the rope. Our crossing started smoothly. The river was muddy, thick and fast. We all had to hang on tight. Splashes of cold, murky water on my face pushed me to question myself about how I got myself into this. But the dream of getting that much closer to my love whom I missed so, so much, made my heart warm and my decision worthwhile. I needed to go on.

Once we approached the middle of the river, the Mexican guy stopped pulling the rope. He looked around and slowly and clumsily pulled a rusty little knife out of his pocket. He then smiled at our surprised and terrified faces and started wielding the knife

"Money, give me money," he yelled with a thick Spanish accent.

I could see that despite his smile, he, too, was absolutely terrified. He knew that he could not wait too long in the water because there was a chance that all of us would be spotted by the border patrol. But he took his chances and once again asked for money.

Before we were brought up to the embankment, we were asked to give them all our money, documents and luggage, so officially we were not supposed to have any money on us. I tried to explain the situation to him. With one hand holding onto the shaky tube, I tried to pull out my empty pocket liner to make him understand that we had no money. By then, we were all soaking wet and everyone, including the Mexican guy, was shivering.

Once again, he wielded the knife and asked for money. Then he pulled his leg out of the tube and started kicking one of the guys right across from him trying to push him into the water. We all started yelling at him and tried to stop him from kicking, but he had a knife and we were all a bunch of scare little puppies. There was no use. Either he didn't understand English or he didn't want an explanation instead of money.

Finally, one of the other guys pulled his leg out of the water, reached into his socks and pulled out a folded twenty-dollar bill. He extended his arm to the Mexican guy.

"This is all I have," he said.

I couldn't believe that twenty dollars was all it took to convince the Mexican guy to continue the journey to the other side of the river. On the other side of the river, the embankment was complimented by a tall fence on top of it. At first, I thought that was the end of the road for us. The fence was at least eight feet tall and very sturdy. But, once we climbed the embankment, I realized that a small portion of the fence was already cut and all we had to do was push it out to be on the other side of the border. As such, we passed through the fence one by one. And just like that, we were in the US for the first time!

Years later, while driving Highway 5 in California with my family going down to San Diego, I noticed the traffic signs that warned drivers about bunches of people running across the freeway. That sign reminded me of that fateful day when we crossed the border into the US. We found ourselves right on the side of Highway 85. Cars were flying by and we were supposed to run across the freeway to meet our next contact. We were all wet and our shoes were slippery. But we didn't come all this way to be stopped by the freeway and waves of speeding cars. I decided to take my chances and, as soon as I saw an opportune moment, I started running. The rest of the guys followed suit, and we all safely crossed the freeway.

On the other side, there was an open space and a bunch of tract homes with their back yards hugging the open space. There was a small passageway to the cul-de-sac on the other side of the tract homes. A taxi cab was waiting for us exactly according to the plan shared with us during our short stay at the Juarez hotel. I felt bad about sitting in the cab with all my wet clothes, but the driver asked us to hurry up and complained that we were late already.

Ahhh, the joy I felt while the cab was driving down the freeway. I was high with the feeling of accomplishment and the thought of getting closer and closer to Farzaneh. At that moment, I felt it was very possible I would see her in just a few days. My perilous journey was almost over.

After a short drive, we were dropped off in front of a Holiday Inn. Jahangir was waiting for us in the parking lot. He smiled as he approached to greet us. He shook our hands and reassured us that it was going to be over very soon.

Chapter 11

USA

The new beginning

It was a nice spring afternoon in El Paso. The year was 1988 and both Juarez and El Paso were far from succumbing to the drug wars that would take over the region two decades later. Our entire group of 25 was successfully transferred from Juarez to El Paso. Each group of three was placed into a nice room at the newly built Holiday Inn on the outskirts of downtown El Paso. I had my first American pizza within a few minutes of checking into our room. Jahangir had made sure we'd have warm meals when we arrived. The television was on and MTV was actually playing music videos. I was so happy and content. I could relax. I was finally done with my journey and I was here in the United States. I was a domestic flight away from San Francisco, where my heart lay waiting for me.

Within a few hours, we were called for a meeting in the lobby of the hotel. Jahangir and a few other older men were there to explain the next step of our trip to various cities across the US. Each of those men was responsible for a specific region. That was when we learned we hadn't actually reached safety yet. The real border between the countries was somewhere outside of El Paso. There were multiple check points across all freeways, roads, and highways leading out of the city of El Paso. After all my troubles, it made sense to me that this one border crossing with no major problems was too good to be true. The real crossing hadn't happened yet. They told us that all bus and train stations, taxi cabs, and airports were subject to extreme inspection. There was no simple way out of El Paso.

From here, their plan was to hollow out a space in the back of a few semi-trucks loaded with fresh produce, making enough room for five or six people. The only benefit of this I could see was that the trucks were cooled to keep the produce fresh, so we wouldn't need to worry about things getting too hot. Once we were a few hundred miles outside of El Paso, the truck would drop us off and we could catch a bus to our final destination.

The trucks would be ready before 8 pm the next day. We would exit the hotel in the dark and jump in the back of the truck. The boxes of fresh produce would provide a visual cover for us at the check points. The aroma of fresh produce was also supposed to confuse the police dogs. Until then, we were to stay our rooms, out of sight, and not go out under any circumstances. Even meals would be delivered to us and we were to stay off of the phones.

After the meeting, everyone was visibly nervous. We'd all just had a few hours of peace before we were bombarded with the bitter truth about the real border of the United States.

The next day was a drag through most of the day. Breakfast and lunch were both delivered to our rooms. By afternoon, we had gone through all the videos MTV had to offer. The other guys I was sharing the room with were dozing off as we waited for dinner to be delivered. It was around 5 pm and I was about done with my last cigarette when I heard a hard knock on the door. It was completely different from the soft knocks the delivery people had used so far. Anxiety zipped through my body like a bolt of electricity, freezing me to my seat.

The second set of knocks was accompanied with a stern voice.

"Open up, Police. Open up, immigration."

I thought about jumping out of the window, but we were on the third floor, and I wasn't sure whether there were any other teams of police outside the window. So, I did all I could do. I opened the door.

A team of five policemen swarmed inside the room yelling, "On the ground, on the ground!"

The other poor bastards jumped out of bed at the noise with dazed and confused looks on their faces as we all went down the floor. In less than a minute, we were in zip tie handcuffs. As I was picked up off the floor, I realized we were being filmed by another policeman who was standing outside the door. He held a huge camera on his shoulder with lights and all. We were moved out of the hotel room and hustled into a black van. I saw Jahangir already in handcuffs sitting inside the van. He looked very sad.

This was getting old. I was again inside a police van with handcuffs going toward some sort of prison. Was I truly doomed to continue returning to prison, again and again, as the old man in Iran had told me?

It seemed like we were traveling for a long drive. Maybe it just seemed long because there were no windows to the outside.

Finally, the van stopped, and we were pulled out. It looked like we were out of the city limits. All I could see around us was dry and lonely desert. Across from the parking lot, there was an old prison compound obviously still in use.

We were directed through three rows of fencing and a revolving metal door. Then I was asked to follow an agent to a room by myself. The room was entirely made of stainless steel, including the floor, ceiling and the bench that was bolted to the ground. It was extraordinarily bright and cold. I was told to sit tight and wait. Within an hour, the same agent came back to the room. He brought a rolling desk holding a VCR and a small TV. He lit a cigarette and offered me one too. I accepted. I had seen this scene in the movies so many times I almost knew how the conversation was going to go.

We were given very special instructions for this specific situation in advance by Jahangir. He told us if we were captured by the border police force, we were to deny the fact that we were brought here with his help. He claimed doing so would complicate the matter further. He also told us to make sure not to tell them the original country we came from. Once they have a country of origin, he said, they could easily deport us back to where we came from. This turned out to be very inaccurate information, but that's another story.

"Do you know a man called Jahangir?" the officer asked me, holding out a photo of Jahangir.

I shook my head no.

"We know this man Jahangir is a human trafficker. We've had him under surveillance for a while now."

I chose to stay silent.

"We decided to move in now because there are so many of you crossing the border. How many people would you say are in your group? You do know this man Jahangir, don't you?"

"I have no idea who you're talking about," I said, as I was told to do.

The officer seemed disappointed and somewhat bored. He got up and turned on the TV and VCR set.

"From the moment you got out of the taxi cab in Juarez, you've been under surveillance," he said. "We knew your every step from Juarez to where you are now."

"Where are we?" I asked.

He looked a little surprised I didn't know.

"You're in an ICE processing facility," he said. At my blank look, he added, "Immigration and Customs Enforcement prison."

Meanwhile, next to him on the TV screen, I could see my entire border crossing through the border patrol camera, including the incident when the Mexican demanded money from us in the middle of the river and tried to kick one of us off the inner tube.

"The taxi cab driver who picked you up in El Paso was actually one of our informants," the officer told me. "We knew exactly what, when, and how you were planning to get out of El Paso. We already know it all. It's useless for you to lie to us. For your own benefit, you need to tell us the truth."

I kept denying that I knew Jahangir and that he was the man who planned and executed our passage into Mexico illegally and then across the border into the US over the border fence above the Rio Grande river. The officer kept asking me to confirm various, frighteningly accurate, details.

it seemed like he had to go through a specific series of questions to properly fill out his report. I sighed and settled back to endure the process more comfortably.

He then asked me, "Where are you coming from?" with a casual look on his face.

“I don’t remember, ah, I’m not sure,” I told him. There was a traitorous nervousness evident in my voice, and I was no longer so relaxed.

“Which country are you coming from?” he asked me again.

“I haven’t slept for days and I had to cross the border and fight with a knife wielding Mexican,” I said with a convincing tone. After all, he’d shown me the film already. I was merely following what I was instructed to say in case of being captured.

“I honestly don’t remember much,” I said to him while squinting my eyes from the reflection of florescent lights bouncing around in that reflective room.

No matter how many times he asked me, I denied everything and told him I did not remember a thing.

“If you don’t cooperate with us, your punishment will be harsher and your time in prison will be longer,” he threatened.

I just looked at him and remained silent.

He wrote a note in a folder with my name on it and left.

A few hours later, another officer took me to the bathroom area. He gave me a pack of clothes to change into, plastic sandals, and a bag. He told me to take a shower and put on the prison attire. I was to fill up the bag with my personal stuff. By then, it was almost midnight. I was directed to a bigger room with rows and rows of bunkbeds filled with sleeping prisoners. He showed me an empty bed and told me the wakeup call was at 4:30 am.

Morning call came way too early. All prisoners were up and running before I even opened my eyes. Guards were yelling constantly for prisoners to hurry up and get to the yard for headcount. It was still dark outside when I tasted my first desert morning chill in the prison yard. After going through the headcount, it was time for bathroom visits and clean up for breakfast.

The bathroom was a collection of 40 toilets in two rows of twenty back to back bowls with absolutely no space in the middle and no dividers whatsoever. Prisoners would take turns sitting on the toilet to take care of their business while everyone else was either sitting next to and behind them or standing in front of them in a line of impatient people waiting to go. I decided to not go to the bathroom until the next chance I was given and maybe the crowd would not be as heavy.

One of the guards stopped me while I was trying to slowly move back out of the crowd of prisoners.

"This will be your only chance to visit the restroom until late afternoon," he warned.

I still wanted to take my chances.

Breakfast was perfect. It consisted of a tray full of fresh breads, jam, peanut butter, coffee and a cup of milk per prisoner. Even fruit was included in our morning diet. After that, we were all counted again and left in the yard for the entire day. The typical day consisted of playing volleyball, working with weights or just walking around. Prisoners were also allowed to just sit and chat. Unlike the Hollywood movies, there were no fights or gangs. No one was planning to escape or making knives out of spoons and pencils to attack and kill other prisoners.

On the third day, I was allowed to make a phone call. That was my chance to finally call Farzaneh and let her know of my whereabouts. Clearly, everyone was extremely worried about me and, until that day, no one knew what had happened to me. The short time I was allowed to speak to her on the phone did not allow me to tell her the entire story, but it was enough for her to know that I was finally here in the US. She was crying and laughing at the same time. Although I was in prison, it seemed like the misery of being away from her was about to end. This wasn't like the unending torture of prison in Iran or the horrible conditions of prison in Cuba. This was just another step I needed to take. I was very happy and somewhat nervous about the near future.

The next day I was called into the warden's office and met a man who introduced himself as my lawyer. He was hired by Jahangir to represent all of us in front of the judge. The man told me he would try to get bail set at a lower rate and transfer my next court date to the San Francisco court of immigration.

Two weeks passed, and I got to know a few other people in the prison who came from different parts of the world. They all shared a similar story. Theirs were stories of constant struggle with relentless poverty, joblessness, and an absolute lack of security for them as well as their family in the original country they escaped from. Their stories reminded me about what I had gone through since my teenage years. I felt their pain and suffering. Mine was a similar story that had flourished into a love story. I had to cross the oceans and travel through continents to reach her. Literally. But here I was, only one step away from completing that journey.

Finally, I heard from the office that I was to attend court that afternoon. I was transferred, along with five other prisoners, to a small courtroom within the same facility. We waited outside the courtroom for a few hours. By late afternoon, the lawyer came out of the courtroom with his stereotypical briefcase filled with folded paper and binders.

"Your bails are set at $3,500 each," he said. "You'll be freed on bail in a few days."

For me, I would be required to show up in the San Francisco immigration court within the next six months. The other prisoners were told something similar, each having to show up at immigration court at their final destinations.

This was great news as far as I was concerned, and I could finally see the light at the end of the tunnel. In a few days, my tumultuous journey was going to reach its happy ending. During these last few days in the El Paso prison, I had time to reflect on my entire journey and see myself as the new man I had become. I thought about how I was going to find a job, go to school, and build my future with Farzaneh. I fantasized about the moment I would see her again for the first time after so many months of perilous journey and adverse incidents along the way. I was in heaven those last few days in that El Paso jail and I was flying through fantasies of my near future.

Pacing back and forth under the relentless sun of El Paso in the prison yard, I remembered the day I was denied my student visa by the American Consulate in Ankara. I realized that day made me even stronger in my decision to follow my love. That day, for a brief moment, I thought our love story had ended. Everything seemed like a losing game. But that moment passed quickly and now I was here, only a short flight away from my new life with her.

The day of my freedom finally arrived. I was called after breakfast to the warden's office and given my clothes and belongings.

Then I was dropped off at the airport. And I was free in the United States!

I didn't know how to feel about that moment in time. My journey was over. I had achieved what I was planning for months. I was here at last. It is a strange feeling when the sheer desire of being somewhere impossible with the one you love so desperately becomes secondary to the mission of how to get there. For the past several months, I had done nothing but planning and executing to get me to this moment. The successes and failures along the way required all my attention and energy to get me through but now, I was here. Now, my real life would finally begin. Now, I had to plan for a life together with someone who I longed to be with. Forever.

Two short flights got me to San Francisco. It was late evening. I got off the plane and walked through the hallway toward the arrivals gate. There she was. Standing in the baggage collection area with her beautiful smile. Her gorgeous eyes were shining across the hallway. I recognized her older sister standing next to her and a huge crowd of passengers swarming around the baggage carousel, but all that crowd faded into blurry back ground and it was as if Farzaneh was standing there alone. I walked as fast as I could toward her. My heart was pumping faster than ever. Or maybe it had stopped. I was breathless and really couldn't tell. She was only a few feet away from me. It did not feel real until I held her in my arms and did not let go. I was here with her, finally.

A few years passed before my heart beat as fast as that awesome night at the airport. That was the night I held Farzaneh's hand in mine in a hospital room in Berkeley. The feeling was exactly the same as when I arrived in San Francisco for the first time. Only this time, she was giving birth to our daughter Leila.

Throughout her pregnancy, rubbing her belly and feeling the occasional kick as the baby grew was the ultimate pleasure of being a new dad. When it came down to the time of giving birth, I could hardly breathe. It was a nerve-racking few hours for me and an absolutely painful one for Farzaneh. At 8:35 pm, on a peaceful summer Sunday which just happened to be Father's Day, Leila was born. I could hardly stay on my feet when I saw my daughter for the first time. She was beautiful. She cried for a short time while they were cleaning her, but then the magic happened. As soon as they put her onto Farzaneh's chest, she got quiet and, with her eyes wide open, she looked around the room. At that moment and from then on, I was and have been the happiest man in the world. I had my very own beautiful family at last.

When I was younger, I constantly questioned my existence and tried so hard to decipher the reasons behind it. I tried religions and philosophies; I read several books and essays. I joined religious groups and practiced with Sufis and Dervishes. I spent days and months searching for the reason. Why was I here?

That night, when my little daughter held my finger tightly in her soft, chubby little hand and didn't let go, I finally got my answer. I was here for this moment. I was here to have shared in the creation of such a precious little angel with the woman I loved more than life. My whole life, I was surrounded by never-resting monsters whom I fought both within and around me. I carried them in my soul and memories all those years. Most of my younger years, I was pushed around, tortured and persecuted by those monsters. All the while, they were the ones pushing me through my life's path to arrive at that moment in my existence, to give me the strength and determination to keep going. The moment that became the ultimate joy in my life. Sharing my love, my heart and my life with my wife and beautiful daughter.

I was so grateful. And all at once, I was no longer bitter and afraid about my memories of those horrible inner demons. Because they had brought me to this life, this happiness, here, they suddenly became my beloved monsters.

Made in the USA
San Bernardino, CA
07 February 2020